ULTRA FUCKERS

CARLTON MELLICK III

ERASERHEAD PRESS
PORTLAND, OREGON

ERASERHEAD PRESS
205 NE BRYANT
PORTLAND, OR 97211

WWW.ERASERHEADPRESS.COM

ISBN: 1-62105-038-6

AUTHOR'S NOTE

The Japanese are the greatest thing to ever happen to this planet. Without them, I probably wouldn't even bother waking up in the morning. Just thinking about their music, movies, and culture makes me so happy that I want to put tiny windmills on my nipples and run around a grocery store singing the Digimon theme song at the top of my lungs. If anyone feels the same way about the Japanese and wants to do this with me some time, please let me know.

The Ultra Fuckers is an underground Japanese band that I like. However, the Ultra Fuckers in this book really have nothing to do with the real Ultra Fuckers. The Japanese characters in this book are over-embellished caricatures taken from a combination of personalities from the members of Guitar Wolf, Hardcore Dude, The Boredoms, Melt Banana, and a dozen other crazy noise punk bands.

"Ultra Fuckers" is one of the shortest books I've written. This is a good thing, in my opinion. If I can cut a book down to as few pages as possible, I am happy. I'm not a fan of fluff or filler in fiction. As a reader, I hate overwritten books. I like my books to be as lean as possible.

F. Scott Fitzgerald once told Tom Wolfe that all writers fall into two camps: the "putter-inners" and the "taker-outers." The putter-inners (ex: Stephen King, Tom Wolfe, Herman Melville) are writers who try to improve their work by adding more text. Their books tend to be very fat and overly descriptive. They have difficulty deleting text, even if it is useless fluff. The taker-outers (ex: Gustave Flaubert, F. Scott Fitzgerald, Antoine de Saint-Exupery) are those who try to improve their work by deleting text. Their books tend to be slender and tight. They make sure every word counts. But they have difficulty adding and expanding on their work

I am definitely a taker-outer. I firmly believe that less is more. After I write a first draft of a book, I start cutting things. I strip the story down to its bare essence. In my opinion, a book that is supermodel-thin is beautiful.

F. Scott Fitzgerald believed that taker-outers were better than putter-inners. I disagree with this completely. Although I prefer books by taker-outers, I think that both writing methods have their strengths and weaknesses. It also seems that most people prefer fat, overwritten books, judging by the size of books in the bookstores these days, so there's nothing wrong with being a putter-inner.

Of course, if you really think about it, it's bullcrap to place everyone into two black and white categories. I'm sure there are writers who are good (or bad) at both. So I guess we can say that F. Scott Fitzgerald is full of shit. But, then, if you think about it, we can say that all authors are full of shit, including (or especially) me. If you ask me, you're better off just ignoring us egotistical sons of bitches. We should be lucky that you bother to read our books at all.

"Ultra Fuckers" is my second stab at absurdist suburban horror. The first was "Menstruating Mall." This is the kind of horror that I find the scariest. Murderers, zombies, alien creatures, demons… they aren't anything compared to the suburbs. There's nothing that makes my skin crawl more than a clean, brand new, wholesome suburban neighborhood. The Southwestern-style neighborhoods of Arizona where I was raised are especially terrifying.

—Carlton Mellick III, 2/2/2008

CHAPTER ONE

SUBURBAN WASTELAND

Tammy and Tony are waiting outside the entrance of the Eagle Hills gated community; they aren't speaking to one another and they are ten minutes late for a dinner party.

Tammy has the radio vexatiously loud to create a barrier of noise between them, a curtain dividing the car. She doesn't want to hear him flaring his nostrils or sniffing at the air, as she cleans her square glasses with a moist towelette.

Tony frowns at the radio. His wife knows that he can't handle listening to the radio so loud, especially when it's the news. The volume is up so high that he can't even understand what is going on overseas or what corner the president has backed himself into this time. He flares his nostrils at Tammy and then sniffs the air—something he does whenever he's nervous.

The gate attendant is not letting them through. He is sitting there at his post, staring at them with a librarian face. Tony gets out of the car.

"Excuse me," he says to the gate attendant.

The attendant does not move.

"What's wrong with him?" Tony mutters.

Tammy responds by blowing her lenses dry.

"Are you sure this is the right place?" Tony asks.

Tammy responds by closing the driver's side door to stop the air conditioning from leaking out. Her husband untucks his shirt at her and approaches the security post. He pulls out a folded piece of paper and presses it face-forward against the plexiglass.

"I've got the passcode but I'm not sure where I'm supposed to enter it," he tells the gate attendant.

The attendant just stares forward with his librarian face.

"Hello?" Tony taps the plexiglass to get his attention. Nothing.

Tony stands there holding up the passcode at the motionless man until Tammy honks the horn at them. As soon as the horn sounds, the gate opens. Tammy continues honking until Tony tucks his shirt back in and returns to the car.

"We're late," she says, but Tony can't hear her over the blaring newscaster.

This is the first time Tony has ever gone with Tammy to one of her company's social functions. He wanted to watch the hockey game during the company picnic. He wanted to drink himself stupid with his old college buddies during the company Christmas party. He pretended to be ill on her company's family bowling night. He said he had to work late every single time her co-workers invited them out for drinks after work. But Tony couldn't wiggle his way out of this one. Tammy's boss has a special dinner planned for tonight. He insisted that all married couples bring their spouses. Tammy would never forgive him if he ruined this for her.

"Why do you even bother going to these things?" Tony always asks.

"Because I have to," Tammy always responds.

"Why? You don't get paid to go to them. You don't even like any of these people."

"You don't understand. If I don't go they'll think that I'm not serious about my job."

"It's not like you'd get fired for skipping the company picnic."

"They want their employees to take an outside interest in the company. The job has to be more than just a paycheck to us."

"How can working in benefits for a cell phone company be more than just a paycheck to anyone?"

"That's how the corporate world works. You have to make everyone believe that you love your job and are proud to be working for your company. You have to make friends with your coworkers and take an interest in their lives outside of work. You have to ask them about their children and laugh at their jokes. You don't have to always socialize with your boss and coworkers outside of work, but you have to *want* to always socialize with your boss and coworkers outside of work."

"Why can't you just go to work, do a good job, and go home?" Tony always asks.

"You just don't get it," Tammy always responds.

Tony has never worked in the corporate world. He likes to work with his hands. He owns his own landscaping business and works out of his truck. His employees are a couple Tongans and a couple high school football players. The only problem with the Tongans is that they don't know much English and the only problem with the high school kids is that they always bug him to buy them beer. Tony rectified these problems by having the Tongans buy the teenagers their beer and having the teenagers be the ones who communicate with the Tongans. It's not fun working at the crack of dawn but he loves finishing his day at lunch time.

Though not a fan of upper middleclass tract housing developments like Eagle Hills, Tony has done his share of landscaping jobs for similar communities. Because every yard of every house in these communities use the same materials and the same basic layout, the planners don't need to hire professional landscapers for these projects. They prefer to hire workers from cheaper independent companies like Tony's.

It's not that Tony doesn't appreciate the work, but every time he helps create one of these cookie-cutter neighborhoods it's like he's giving up a tiny piece of his soul. The houses have no history or character, no imagination or flavor. They just seem bland and lifeless, much like the people who live inside them.

Two things Tony never wanted for his life were to

work in the corporate world or to live in a cookie-cutter house.

Once inside the gates of Eagle Hills, Tony notices many empty lots near the entrance containing half a dozen bulldozers and stacks of construction materials. Tammy said this development is new, but she never said it was still under construction. He wonders if Tammy's boss might be able to get him in touch with the housing planner to see if they need some extra landscapers. If he could get some new work out of it, this dinner party might not be such a waste after all.

The neighborhood looks the same as all the other housing developments he has worked on outside of Scottsdale. They all have that same hideously pseudo-Southwestern style, with sunset-colored gravel yards, Palo Verde trees, pueblo-colored roof tiles, and rough stucco paint jobs, all of which are somehow supposed to appear deserty...even though none of these materials can be found naturally in this desert.

All of the houses seem pretty empty. Most of them probably haven't sold yet. They pass a few houses with cars in their driveways, but they don't see any people or anyone else driving on the road.

Tony turns off the radio.

"Okay, now where is this place?"

Tammy opens her purse and casually flips through

her belongings for the address.

"Come on, come on," Tony grunts.

Tammy doesn't search any faster.

"Why did you put the directions back in your purse?"

"I didn't want to lose them," she says, continuing her search.

Tony stops the car in the middle of the road.

"Why are you stopping?" Tammy asks.

"I'm waiting for you."

"Keep driving. We're already late."

"I'm not going anywhere until I know where I'm supposed to go. I don't want to get lost in this place."

"You're blocking traffic," she says.

"Do you see anyone else on the road?" he says.

"Just GO!" Tammy says, stomping a high-heeled shoe on Tony's foot.

Tony pushes her away. "Fine, I'm going. You big baby."

Tammy notices the party invitation is now in her lap. It must have been stuck to the bottom of her purse the whole time.

"Here," she says, throwing the directions at him.

"Don't give them to me, read them," Tony says.

"*You* read them."

"I'm driving."

"Yeah, at 2 miles an hour. You drive like an old man."

Tony flares and unflares his nostrils several times until Tammy turns the radio back on and separates them by the curtain of noise.

The address is 26H7K SE Pueblo. Tony wonder's why the address has letters in them. He wonders if it is a typo.

Tony can't read any of the addresses printed on the sides of the brick mailboxes along the side of the road. The twilight sun is shining in their eyes. He turns the radio down.

"Help me find the place. I can't read the addresses."

"You're so blind," Tammy says, taking the directions away from him.

"Just read one of them for me."

Tammy tries to read one of them.

"Well?" he asks.

"Ummm…" Tammy rolls down her window and leans in to get a better look.

"Read it already."

"I can't… "

"Christ." Tony stops the car.

"They're not even addresses," Tammy says.

Tony opens his door and leans closer to a mailbox. The numerals on the side of the mailbox are just five gold zeroes with lines through them. He looks at a front door. No address. He looks at a curb. Nothing there either. It's like every house has the same address: 00000.

"Maybe they haven't given the houses addresses yet," Tammy says.

"They give houses addresses before they're even built."

"Well, I don't know. Just keep going. Maybe I'll recognize someone's car."

Tony drives on.

"What road is this?" Tammy asks as they approach the intersection.

"Pueblo Drive," Tony says.

"I thought we were already on Pueblo... "

"We're on Pueblo Blvd. This is Pueblo Drive."

"They live on Pueblo."

"Which Pueblo? Blvd or Drive?"

"It doesn't say."

They keep driving.

"Just read me the directions," Tony says.

"They say turn right on Pueblo. We did that. It will be the second house after P. Circle."

"Why didn't you just say so?" Tony says. "We don't need the address as long as we can find P. Circle."

They continue down the road for twenty minutes, keeping an eye out for P. Circle. They pass Pueblo Court, Pueblo Mountain Road, Old Pueblo Way, New Old Pueblo Way, Pueblo Sunset Ridge, Sunset Pueblo Ridge, Pueblo Cactus Road, St. Pueblo Cactus Street, Los Pueblos Drive, Sunset Cactus Pueblo Court, Pueblo Creek Road, Cactus Mountain Pueblo New Sunset Ridge Place, and Cactus Sunset Drive (AKA Pueblo Street).

After that, the road curves and becomes Pueblo Street. Then the road ends at Pueblo Circle.

"Is this P. Circle?" Tony asks.

"I guess P. could stand for Pueblo."

"But the road ends here," Tony says. "It's supposed to be two houses after P. Circle."

"Turn right," Tammy says. "I'm sure it's around here somewhere."

Tony does as she says.

Pueblo Circle curves into Old Pueblo Circle. Tony doesn't understand how there can be an *old* version of Pueblo Circle since both of them were created at the same time only months ago. They arrive at another street called Pueblo Drive, then another street called Pueblo Circle, then another street called Pueblo Blvd. They aren't sure if these are the same streets they have seen before or if they are new streets with the exact same names. They turn on Pueblo.

"This is absolutely ridiculous," Tony says. "How in the world do they expect anyone to find their way around in here?"

"I can't believe how late you're making us," Tammy says.

"Oh, please," Tony says. "You're the one with the directions."

"You're doing this on purpose." Tammy says. "You're just trying to wiggle your way out of going to this dinner party."

"If I knew it was going to take us this long to find the place I never would have agreed to come," Tony says. "I mean, come on, everything looks *exactly* the same here. I don't know how anyone could ever find their way around in this place, even if they lived here."

"I knew you'd ruin this for me somehow," Tammy says.

They drive in circles for another forty minutes, turning on the same roads or similar-sounding roads, driving up and down block after block searching for cars that Tammy recognizes. So far, they haven't seen many cars in the neighborhood at all. Tammy is looking for Gina's red mini-cooper or George's black BMW, but the few automobiles they have seen were either silver SUVs or silver 4-door sedans.

"I'm going to have to call him," Tammy says, taking her cell phone out of her purse.

"You could have called him this whole time?" Tony says.

"I didn't realize his number was on the invitation," she says.

Tony groans. "What a bonehead."

She programs his phone number into her speed dial and clicks *send*.

"He's going to be so mad that we're late," she says.

"No, he's not, Tammy," Tony says.

"You don't understand how critical he is about this kind of stuff," Tammy says, listening to her cell phone.

"Well, tough beans."

"You see," she says, closing her cell phone and dropping it onto the back seat. "He's turned his phone off.

He's got to be pissed."

"Yeah, right," Tony says under his breath.

Tammy turns on the radio full blast but there is only static. She switches the station to some classic guitar music, but there is a lot of static bleeding into this channel as well so she just turns it off.

Tony stretches his neck over the steering wheel and makes a bulldog face until Tammy laughs. Tony knows that making funny faces is the easiest way to cheer her up. But her smile quickly turns to a frown as Tony unintentionally sniffs at the air again.

CHAPTER TWO

HERE YOUR
POP FOOD

Tammy and Tony are driving aimlessly through the streets of the Eagle Hills gated community; the sun has gone down and they are seventy-eight minutes late for a dinner party.

"Try calling again," Tony says. "Leave a message."

"I don't want him to know we've been driving in circles for over an hour," she says. "I'm going to tell him we had car trouble."

"If you don't tell him we're lost how is he going to help us find the place? I'm sure he understands that this place can get more than a little confusing."

"You don't understand," she says. "If I tell him we're lost it means that it was my fault and that I can't follow directions properly. But if I tell him we had car trouble, then it is the car's fault."

"But wouldn't having an unreliable car also make you look bad? If he can tell you're lying won't that make you look even worse? Besides it wasn't your fault he gave us crummy directions."

Tammy calls and leaves him a message. She says that there was an accident on the freeway and that she will be there any minute.

"He's still not answering," Tammy says.

"Why'd he put his phone number on the invitation if he wasn't going to answer his phone?"

"He probably would have answered the phone if we called him before seven."

25

"Well, call Gina. You have her phone number don't you?"

"I keep all of their business cards in my wallet," she says. "But I think they only list their work numbers and their work email addresses."

"With your company, I'm surprised they don't force you to program everyone's home phone numbers into your cells."

"I wish they would have," she says.

Another twenty minutes goes by.

"Call him again," Tony says. "We're never going to find it otherwise."

"I can't tell him we're lost now," she says. "I already told him an accident made us late."

"Well, it's possible that an accident made us late and we also couldn't find the place."

"Do you know how bad it sounds to have two excuses?"

"No matter how probable they are?"

"George doesn't buy excuses, even when they're true. Remember the time I had food poisoning and he assumed I just wanted to have a three day weekend?"

"The guy's an idiot," Tony says. "It's his fault we're late. If you don't call him I'm going to."

"You can't call him. He doesn't know you."

"I don't care. I'm hungry and I'm sick of this."

"Dinner's probably almost over by now."

"Then why don't we just go home?"

"We're not going home. I already told him we were almost there. We have to at least show up so I can save face. I don't care if we're only there for desert."

"I should've gotten a burger while you were getting ready," Tony says. "I've been starving for hours."

"You don't eat ten minutes before a dinner party, you pig," Tammy says. "You're not supposed to eat that crap anyway."

Tony imitates the hungry whimper of a hound dog. He always does that to be cute when Tammy won't let him eat the food he wants.

Another hour passes.

They drive slowly through the dimly lit streets of Eagle Hills. It looks like there are people living in all of these homes. Every house has their porch light on and every living room window glows with the jumpy yellow light of television sets.

They come across a house that doesn't fit with the others. It is the only building with a hint of uniqueness. It's constructed with the same materials as the other houses, the same gravel yard, the same stucco walls, the same windows. Only instead of where a garage would be there is a drive-thru window. Instead of a mailbox there is a cactus-shaped sign that reads "Eagle Hills Pop Food" in a fancy yet deserty font, with the silhouette of a howling coyote head. A spot light shines on an *open* sign above the front door. Though it says it is open, there doesn't seem to be any signs of life.

Tony stops in front of the building.

"What is it?" Tammy asks.

"Looks like an independent fast food franchise," Tony says.

"What is it doing here?"

"This place is so big and out of the way that they probably need their own restaurants and stores."

Tony drives the car into the driveway.

"What are you doing?" Tammy asks.

"Getting some food. I'm hungry."

He follows the driveway around the back of the house where the back yard should have been. Instead, there is a mini-parking lot and a food menu.

"You can't eat now. We need to find the place."

"I'm starving," Tony cries.

"Can't you wait, porky?" Tammy says.

"No," he says. "If we missed dinner, I'm eating now."

"We won't be there long. Wait until the way home."

"It'll take two minutes."

"God, you're such a pain."

The drive-thru menu doesn't look as commercial as a normal fast food place. It looks more like a church's event calendar. There is everything from cheeseburgers to chicken sandwiches to pizza to burritos to hotdogs to chili cheese tater tots.

The intercom system is more like the kind you would find in a house rather than on a fast food menu. Tony reaches his hand out the window and holds the button in as he speaks.

"Ummm… hello?" he says.

He releases the button but there's only static.

"Are they even open?" Tammy asks.

Tony hushes her. He pushes the button down and speaks loudly into the intercom. "I'd like a bacon cheeseburger, a fish taco, a large curly fry, a large coke, and… " He turns to Tammy. "Do you want anything?"

She grinds her fist at him and shakes her head. Then spits and pouts into her purse.

"That'll be it," he says.

He waits for a response. Only static.

"Nobody's there, dumbshit."

"Somebody's there… " Tony says.

He drives around the side of the house to the payment window. It isn't actually a window, more like a drive-thru ATM. On the screen there is a list of the items he ordered and a total. There is a flashing green light telling him to "slide card now." Tony slides his visa debit card through the slot. The blinking light says "thank you" and then "please pull forward" as a receipt prints for him.

The pickup window is also not a window. It looks more like a microwave door on the side of the house. On the microwave there is a sign the reads "Your order will be ready in:" and then there is a counter. Only 16 seconds left. As soon as it counts down to zero, the door pops open and a tray holding a large white drink and a large white bag slides out toward the car window. There's still not a sign of any employees. No sound coming through the walls.

"It's all automated," Tony says.

"It's probably horrible," Tammy says.

Tony grabs the bag and plops it on his lap. The bag has a large smiley face on its front under the words, "Here your pop food!"

Parked on the side of the road, Tony makes a slurping noise while opening his food, which he does whenever he wants to be cute while pigging out. Tammy impatiently checks to make sure her makeup is still intact. She steals glances at her husband's food and groans in disgust.

Tony inhales the cheeseburger and the fries. He notices his wife is glaring at him as he eats.

"What?" Tony asks.

She sneers at him. "Aren't you going to offer me any of your food?"

"Nope," he says. "I already asked if you wanted anything and you said *no*."

"Well, I haven't eaten yet either, you know," she says.

Tony rolls his eyes at her and throws the fish taco at her lap. "Here, you big baby."

"I only want half," she says.

"Just eat it," he says.

She opens the wrapper and rips the taco in half, spreading white sauce all over her fingers.

"God damn it," she says at the white sauce on her fingers.

She hands the fish taco to her husband. White sauce drips onto his pants.

"God damn it," he says to her.

After they finish eating, Tammy calls her boss again. She leaves him a long message stating how Tony has been sick for several days and how he really, really wanted to go to the dinner party to meet everyone, but on the way there he started to get dizzy and had to pull over. He was really trying to make it, but he just wasn't in as good of a condition as he thought he was. She had to take him straight home and put him to bed. She apologized for not calling about it sooner, but she was really worried. She was hoping she could drive him back and still be able to come out to the dinner party herself, but it's just too late now. She suggests they all go out to dinner at the Olive Garden sometime next week, after Tony is feeling better. It takes her twelve minutes just to say goodbye.

"Great story," Tony says.

"I'm going to get fired," Tammy says.

"Don't be ridiculous."

"You wait and see."

Tony is happy they are going home. Though this trip was a huge waste of time, at least he didn't have to meet Tammy's snobbish boss and irritating co-workers. He doesn't know for sure how snobbish or irritating they are, but the stories Tammy brings back with her after work sure do make them sound like horrible people. It's possible that Tammy describes people much differently than they really are. She would describe Tony as a stupid lazy fat slob. But Tony runs his own business, so he can't be that stupid. He wakes up at the crack of dawn to do physical labor every day, so he can't be lazy. He gets a bigger workout in a day than most people get in a month, so he's not fat. And the only reason he's a slob is because he comes home with dirt all over his clothes and doesn't always shower or change into something clean right away.

Tammy doesn't see people realistically. For all Tony knows, her coworkers could be some interesting down-to-earth people. But he kind of doubts it. Even if they are decent human beings in their home life, they'll surely still come off as douchebags by hiding their true personalities for the sake of fitting the behavioral mold that companies expect of their employees. That kind of phony attitude is one thing Tony really hates about the corporate world.

Two things Tony never wanted for his life were to be forced to put on some phony personality for his job or associate with people who use phony personalities because they feel it's expected of them.

"Now we just need to find our way back out of here," Tony says.

They spend an hour trying to find their way out.

"The entrance is on Pueblo Drive, right?" Tony asks.

"No, Pueblo Circle," Tammy says.

"You said the party was at the second house after Pueblo Circle."

"Oh, yeah."

"Or did we start on Pueblo Blvd? Yeah, it was Pueblo Blvd."

They drive street after street, trying to find Pueblo Blvd. None of the streets are familiar, yet they all look the same. They go down Pueblo Place, then Sunset Ridge Pueblo Place, then Old Pueblo Sunset Street, Navajo Pueblo Road, Pueblo Creek Circle, Pueblo Town Circle, Red Pueblo Mountain Way, Navajo Mountain Drive, and Sunset Pueblo Street.

They drive for miles, looking for either Pueblo Blvd or Pueblo Drive. The streets keep going on and on. Tony hits the steering wheel a few times.

"Calm down," Tammy says.

"I can't believe this," he says. "You'd think we would have come across another exit at some point."

"Maybe there's just the one entrance," she says.

"This place is too huge," he says. "There's got to be exits everywhere."

"It's an IQ test," she says. "Figure it out."

"I'd like to see you do better."

She rubs her cheek against the side of the window.

A couple more hours pass. It is getting very late and they are getting very tired.

"Pull over," Tammy says. "Ask someone for directions."

"At this hour?" Tony says. "Everyone's probably asleep. You can't just knock on someone's door. Especially in a neighborhood like this."

"If you would have asked for directions before it wouldn't have been too late."

"No, we just need to keep heading in one direction. Eventually we'll find the outskirts of the community and will be able to get out."

"I'm not waiting any longer," she says. "Pull over. Ask someone for help. If you have to wake them up, then so be it. If they call security, then maybe security will escort us out."

"People really freak out when you bother them in these neighborhoods," Tony says. "You knock on a door in the middle of the night and the next thing you know there's six police cars surrounding you with guns pointed at your head."

"You're such a wimp," she says.

"You do it then, if you're so tough," he says.

Tammy turns the radio back on and blares the static as loud as it can go. Tony pulls over and leaves the car.

He slams the door and approaches one of the houses.

This house has a silver SUV in the driveway, so he knows somebody lives here. Most of the lights are off inside, but there seems to be a kitchen or bedroom light in the distance. Tony looks through the window in the door to see if anyone is awake. But it is very silent and motionless inside. The house is very clean. It is lightly furnished and lightly decorated with a soft southwestern design. He knows he is going to get hell for this, but he rings the doorbell. He presses his forehead through the window, hoping someone will come out of the back room wide awake.

No movement.

He rings the bell again. It is a loud clamor of a bell that reverberates through the vast living room.

A figure sits up from the couch and turns to him. Tony can't see what the person looks like in the darkness of the room. He just sees an outline of a possibly female form.

"I'm sorry to disturb you," he says. "I'm lost and need directions."

The figure doesn't move.

"You can call security and have them assist us if you don't want to open the door," he says. "I understand that it is very late, but we really don't have a choice."

The figure just stares at him.

He continues speaking to her without getting a response. He rings the doorbell again, just in case it isn't really a person at all and his mind is just playing tricks on him. Nobody answers the door. He knocks. He rings again. Nobody comes.

After several minutes of this, he backs up. He returns to the driveway and looks back. The form is watching him through the living room window. He can tell it is definitely a person now.

"Hello?" he says.

The figure steps away from the window and out of view.

When Tony returns to the car, the radio is still on full blast but Tammy is no longer in the front seat. He figures she is just asleep in the back, but when he looks she is not in the car at all.

He opens the car door and turns off the blaring static. Then he looks around the neighborhood. Perhaps she realized Tony wasn't getting anywhere with his inquiry so she's trying a different house herself. Tony walks up the street, checking out all of the houses but he does not see her at any of their front doors. All of the houses are dark and silent. He searches in the opposite direction. Tammy isn't anywhere to be seen. He calls out. No response.

She has been pretty pissed off at him all day, so she might have left the car and stormed down the road. Tony gets back in the car and waits for a while. She doesn't return. He turns the car on and drives around the neighborhood slowly, trying to figure out where should would have gone to. She probably didn't get far.

"Christ," Tony groans.

He knows this is typical Tammy behavior.

He spends the rest of the night, driving up and down the streets, searching for his wife, fading in and out of consciousness. He vows never to try to socialize with Tammy's coworkers ever again. He also vows never to landscape tract housing developments ever again.

CHAPTER THREE

SICK ZIP
EVERYWHERE

Tony wakes up in the back of his car in a parking lot behind another Eagle Hills Pop Food drive-thru; he has a shooting pain in the back of his neck and he is thirteen hours late for a dinner party.

He searched for his wife all night until he just couldn't stay awake anymore and had to pull over and take a nap. He thought it was the same Eagle Hills Pop Food drive-thru he had been to earlier, but it is a different one. They are identical in every way, except the last one was on Pueblo Place and this is Ye Olde Pueblo Drive. He thought sleeping in this parking lot would be better than on the side of the road, because he knows how people in these communities hate when strange cars are parked near their houses.

Tony gets out of the car and stretches out his spine. The bright morning sun blinds him as he crosses the driveway and steps out into the street. He looks to see if anyone is in front of their homes. No one is about. There are no cars driving in the streets. It's a Saturday morning. He wonders why there aren't any children playing outside. Then again, it is summer. Nobody in Arizona goes outside during the summer.

Through the drive-thru, Tony speaks into the intercom at whoever is listening on the other side.

"Hello? Is anyone there?" he asks.

Just static.

"I'm lost and could really use some directions," he says.

"Could you please help?"

Just static.

"Fine," he says. "Just give me some coffee and an egg and bacon sandwich."

He goes back to his car and searches for Tammy's cell phone, just in case she left it behind. He's got to call his employees to tell them why he's late. The phone isn't there. Well, he thinks, at least Tammy won't be stuck out there without a phone. She might have called her sister and got a ride home already. He hopes she feels miserable for what she has done.

He gets in the car and goes through the drive thru. He swipes his card and gets his receipt.

The amount seems kind of high. He looks at what he's ordered:

Coffee $1.27
Breakfast Sandwich $2.76
Directions $3.31
Help $4.98

He's curious about the last two. They aren't food items.

The coffee and bag are already waiting for him as he turns around the corner. He opens the bag and removes the sandwich. At the bottom of the bag there are two envelopes wrapped in the same smiley-faced paper as the food products. Tony opens one of them.

He reads it:

DIRECTIONS

Turn right on Ye Olde Pueblo Drive, turn left on Pueblo Sunset Road, turn left on Apache Mountain Terrace, turn right on Pueblo Town Circle

He sticks his head out of the window.

"Hey, thanks a lot in there!" He smiles and waves at the building. Then he drives out of the lot, following the directions.

He opens the second envelope while eating his microwaved breakfast sandwich.

It reads:

HELP

Beware the cyclops.

"What's that supposed to mean?" Tony says, crumpling the paper and tossing it into the back.

Tony follows the directions perfectly. He has no problems finding the roads he has to turn on. The directions are much easier than the ones to the dinner party.

On Pueblo Town Circle, Tony gets excited to finally be leaving Eagle Hills. He vows never to return to this place ever again. It is, perhaps, the most disgusting neighborhood he has ever visited and he hopes the entire thing burns to the ground.

But instead of an exit out of Eagle Hills, he arrives at a small suburban park at the end of Pueblo Town Circle. The pop food drive-thru didn't give him directions to the exit; it gave him directions to the park. He should have been more specific with where he wanted to go.

There are people in the park. Children playing on the swings and merry-go-rounds. Fathers lounging on picnic blankets. Mothers breast-feeding their babies. All relaxing in the Saturday morning sun, getting some rays before the heat becomes unbearable as it surely will later in the day. The place isn't as lifeless as Tony thought. These are real people doing real people things. Still, they are awfully quiet. They don't seem happy or excited about anything. The children aren't screaming or laughing at each other. Everyone is just staring into space with blank librarian faces.

Tony passes a little girl on the swing. She's wearing a sunny yellow dress. Her hair is blonde, but her facial features are Asian. She looks to be about six years old.

"Hi, there," Tony says to her as he walks through the playground sand.

She ignores him, staring straight forward without a blink.

A boy runs through the sand past Tony. Perhaps eight or nine years old. He too has an Asian face, but with short blond hair. He wears a white short-sleeved button down shirt tucked into black jeans. The boy jumps on a merry-go-round with two girls. Both girls look identical to the girl on the swing. They are the same age, the same height, they wear the exact same yellow dress. Like they are triplets or clones.

Tony steps out of the sand. Another boy and another girl sit in the grass in front of him, completely indistinguishable from the kids on the merry-go-round. They look at him with librarian faces. He decides to keep his distance.

"Excuse me," he says to two adults sitting on a picnic blanket.

The man looks like an older version of the young boy, wearing the same black pants and white shirt. The woman also looks like an adult version of the little girls, wearing a matching yellow summer dress. She is casually nursing a baby. The infant's mouth is open against the side of her breast, but it seems to be uninterested or bored with the nipple.

They move their faces toward the sound of Tony's voice, but they don't look him in the eyes. Even though they are facing him, it's as if they are looking through him rather than at him.

"I'm lost," he says. "Can you tell me the way back to the freeway?"

They stare at him with librarian faces.

"I've been driving aimlessly for hours," he says. "Please. I don't know what to do."

Their gazes wander away from him. He storms away and approaches two duplicates of the woman strolling down a sidewalk. They look at each other and look forward then look back at each other then blink, like they are having a conversation but neither of them are actually talking.

"Ladies, can you help me?" Tony asks.

They don't reply.

He stands in their path. They stop. Both of them look at him then look away then look at each other then look at him then blink. Like he is now apart of their conversation even though none of them are actually talking.

"I need to find my way home," Tony says.

They continue looking around, but do not speak. He steps out of their path and they continue on their path. They look at each other and look forward then look back at each other then blink.

Tony decides to get as far away from these people as he can and try to get the hell away from this neighborhood as quickly as possible. This isn't a normal gated community. There is something genuinely wrong going on here. It's like a secret government project created for testing clones or maybe androids. But what about Tammy's boss? Was he a clone or an android? No, he's not even sure if they entered the right gated community. These places all look alike. Perhaps that's why the government chose such a community for their secret experiment. Unless you live in the community or know someone who lives in the community, you'll never know what actually goes on beyond the gates.

Driving madly down Pueblo Town Circle, Tony decides to just head in one direction. He goes south. Once Pueblo Town Circle comes to an end, he turns right on any road and takes the next left so that he can keep heading south. Eventually he'll get to the outskirts of the neighborhood. Eventually he'll get out.

No matter how far south he drives, the neighborhood never seems to end. He passes the exact same house after house after house. Eventually, his gas drops deep into the red. He pulls over at the next Eagle Hills Pop Food drive-thru. He orders water, a slice of olive pizza, and directions to the nearest exit out of Eagle Hills.

Once he gets the directions, his jaw goes slack. The directions are ten pages long, listing about one hundred streets to turn onto per page. This has got to be some kind of error. He tries ordering directions again, this time wording it a little more clearly. He receives the same directions as before, only one page longer. His request must have confused whoever or whatever is inside of the building.

He goes around to the front of the place and knocks on the front door.

"I need to speak to you," he says.

There isn't a reply. He is surprised to see that the door is unlocked when he turns the knob. But as he opens the door, he realizes that it isn't real. The door is just a decoration on the front of the house. There is only a stucco wall on the other side. The windows, too, are just decorations. There are only curtains separating the wall from the framed glass. Tony circles the building, but there isn't a single entrance. He doesn't understand this. Even if the place was completely automated, there would still need to be an entrance for maintenance workers.

Somebody would have to restock the food within.

Perhaps there is a way to enter the building from under the ground, Tony wonders. But he decides not to look for a way under ground. It's not that important.

As the sun glares down on him, he decides to sit in the car and run the air-conditioning until the gas is out. Then he runs the air-conditioning until the battery dies. Then he relaxes in the cool air until the sun heats it up again. Then the car becomes an oven and he has to get out.

Tony orders five waters from the drive-thru. He drinks one and dumps the others over his head. He goes back to the car and waits for the sun to go down. He orders dinner and eats it on the sidewalk. There aren't any ants or flies to bother him. This place is too sterile for bugs.

He thinks about Tammy. He wonders if it's possible that she actually made it back home. He wonders if she's still out there somewhere, wandering the streets, wishing she didn't run out on her husband the way she did. He wonders if something terrible has happened to her.

Not knowing what else to do, he climbs into the back of his car and goes to sleep. The neighborhood doesn't make a single sound throughout the night.

Tony gets up an hour before the sun. He eats breakfast and then sets out on foot, preparing to follow the very long directions to get out of Eagle Hills. He doesn't believe the directions are really going to take him where he wants to go, but he doesn't know what else to do. He can't sit in his car forever, waiting to be rescued.

The sun beats down on him after two hours of walking and he has just now reached the first turn. After another hour of walking in the direct sunlight, Tony's legs become sluggish. His brain feels cooked. Sweat is caking up on his neck and staining his clothes. He smells like beef stew.

He stops walking once his eyes become sunburned. He's not sure if it is an illusion, but one of the houses up ahead seems to be different from the others. Just slightly different. He moves in closer, trying to ignore the blisters on the bottom of his feet.

The house is the same as the others except for its garage door. Something is written on it. In red spray paint, someone has written "Sick Zip Everywhere" in large crude lettering. He doesn't know what that means, but at least it is something different for a change.

He decides to knock on the door. Perhaps a normal person lives in this one.

No response.

He gets dizzy standing there.

"Fuck it," Tony mumbles.

He picks up a potted cactus from the walkway and throws it at the window on the front door. The glass cracks in two. He takes off his shoe and smashes the glass with the heel until there's not a shard left. Then he reaches his arm through and unlocks the door.

Inside, a woman is sitting on the couch watching the television. She is identical to the other women in this neighborhood. Asian face, blonde hair, yellow summer dress. Tony doesn't bother trying to communicate with her. He sits down next to her and sighs as the air conditioning blows against his neck. She looks over at him and then back at the television. She picks up the remote and then flips through a few channels and then hands the remote to Tony.

Tony flips through the channels as well, but every channel is the same. They all play an Eagle Hills real estate infomercial with Japanese subtitles. He turns it off and sighs. The couch is beige-colored imitation leather and feels like it was purchased from the manufacturer only yesterday. Everything in the house looks like it was purchased only yesterday. From the big screen TV, to the cactus-shaped lamps, to the tan and white carpeting, to the stone-colored coffee table, to the tacky dreamcatchers on the wall. It's all in perfect order, as if no one has ever lived here before.

After he feels like he can get back on his feet, Tony goes upstairs. He takes a shower and shaves. He enters the master bedroom and discovers the closet is filled with identical yellow dresses, white shirts, and black pants. Tony tries on the clothes. He can't fit into the jeans, but he can wear the white shirt. He can also fit into clean underwear and socks.

He stares at himself in the mirror and combs his hair. He thinks about Tammy and wishes she was here with him. Even in this crazy neighborhood, at least they could have been together. He's not sure what is happening to him, but he no longer feels like he is living in the real world.

Two things Tony never wanted for his life were to lose touch with reality or feel completely and utterly alone.

CHAPTER FOUR

JET
WALK

Tony is driving a silver sedan down Pueblo Canyon Road; he has gone one third of his trip toward the nearest exit out of the Eagle Hills gated community and he is fifty-six hours and twenty-two minutes late for a dinner party.

Tony has taken to calling the odd clone-like people that live in Eagle Hills the *mundanes.* Whatever the mundanes are, they don't seem to notice him as he breaks into their houses, sleeps in their beds, and steals their cars. Their kitchens and their refrigerators are empty, so it's too bad that he can't steal their food as well. He has to eat pop food whenever he comes across one of the automated drive-thru buildings, but they aren't as easily accessible as breaking into the houses. Water is more important than food, especially in the heat, so at least he can get water from the mundanes.

There are always the same people in every house. A mom, a dad, a daughter, a son, a baby. They also have a dog, a cat, and a goldfish. Not a single detail is ever different in any of the houses. Sometimes there is a family member, a pet, or a car missing, but nothing new is ever found in these houses. Every time he runs low on fuel, he just pulls over and takes a new car out of any garage. Whenever he has to sleep, he just pulls over and uses one of their beds.

It's taking its toll on his sanity, seeing the same houses over and over again, the same streets, the same emotionless people. But he'll be fine as long as he follows the directions, as long as he is making some kind of progress and has some kind of goal he can reach. As long as he can eventually someday get out of here, he'll be alright.

Troy stops for a burger. He orders fries and a coke. He decides to ask for some help as well.

He keeps driving while he eats. After the fries are done, he unwraps the note card and reads it:

HELP

**Don't stop again until you reach the exit.
The cyclops is following you.**

He tosses the card behind him. For some reason, this warning seems much less like a joke than the previous one. A cyclops doesn't sound very threatening to him. It seems too cartoonish of a creature to actually be frightening, even if they did exist. But the fact that the card knew Tony was heading toward the exit and the fact that something might be following him, does make him a bit nervous. He looks in the rearview mirror, but there aren't any other cars on the road. There hasn't been a single car on the road since he originally arrived in Eagle Hills.

Still, he does have the feeling that he is being followed. It might just be paranoia, but he doesn't feel like he's alone with the mundanes anymore.

Tony turns onto a road that makes him jerk his head back like whiplash. The street is so different from the others that it startled him. The street wasn't designed any different from the others, but it has been completely vandalized. Mailboxes have been torn out of the ground. Tire tracks rip through the landscaping. Windows are smashed. Doors have been pulled off of hinges. Cars are smashed through living rooms. Graffiti is spray-painted all over the place.

Driving slowly through the wreckage of street, he examines the graffiti on the road. It is the same crude red lettering that spelled "Sick zip everywhere" a couple days before. On cars, on driveways, in the street, on windows, there is graffiti everywhere. Many of them read "sick zip" or "headache power." Others read "moshing fuckers here" or "oi! ultra fuckers." One reads "surf punk rock and roll!" and one reads "ultra punk lifestyle." But the most common graffiti reads "ultra fuck you!"

The area doesn't look like it's been vandalized too recently. The mundanes didn't care enough to clean up the street or repair the damage. They probably went on watching their televisions with blank librarian faces.

Tony reaches a less vandalized portion of street. The

neighborhood is less trashed down here. He turns on Pueblo River Lane as per his directions and the neighborhood seems normal again. He's not sure what the vandalism was all about, but he's pretty sure there is at least one other person lost in this godforsaken place. Whoever they are, he hopes he doesn't run into them. They seem to have gone completely insane trying to find their way out.

Tony wonders if he will become just as insane if he doesn't get out.

"Will I succumb to madness and mindlessly destroy everything I come across?" he wonders.

"Hell, yes," he says to himself. "I would tear this place to the ground."

After an hour, Tony comes across another section of Eagle Hills that has been vandalized. The graffiti on the houses reads "punk fuckers!" and "ultra fuck you!" and "ultra crazy mohawk powers!"

Thirty minutes later, he finds another house that's been damaged by these punks. Then, a couple blocks down, there are a few more. Tony thinks there has to be more than one person doing this. He also thinks they have to be some kind of weird punk anarchists. On one house, he sees the words "we're ultra fuckers" and "ultra fuck you!"

"You ultra fuckers must be on crack," he says to the graffiti.

Then he sees this spray painted on the sidewalk: "ultra fuckers on crack! Crazy!"

Further down the road, the vandalized houses become more common than the unvandalized houses. The damage also seems to be more recent. Perhaps even hours ago. The crashed vehicles are still smoking. There are bloodied bodies in the street: dead women in ripped apart yellow dresses, decapitated men and children. These people are more demented than Tony thought.

He keeps driving. Up ahead there are houses on fire. He does not turn around. He has to follow the directions no matter where they take him. If he gets lost again he may never find his way out. Dead animals are piled up in the road, Tony drives through them. A sedan is tipped on its side in the middle of the road, Tony drives up on the sidewalk and goes around it.

He sees a woman in one of the houses watching him. She looks like one of the Asian-faced mundanes but she wears a black and red vinyl dress and has a mohawk made of wiggling goldfish. Tony stares at her and she smiles back. She's not a mundane at all. She's got emotions. She's got freewill. She's got... only one eye.

Tony is too distracted to notice the SUV as it barrels down the street toward him.

The SUV rams into the side of the sedan and crushes it against a nearby driveway.

Tony shakes his head out of shock to the sound of a screeching punk rock noise band. His ribs have bruised under the seatbelt and his knee is swelling after colliding with the dashboard. He takes a look around. The SUV that hit him is covered in spray-paint. Besides more crude sayings, there are pictures of anarchy symbols and mohawks and several angry demonic versions of Pac-Man.

A drunken Asian guy drops out of the driver's side door holding a bloody nose. He wears a leather jacket with chains and studs on it. His hair is spiked in every direction.

"Huh?" says the Asian guy. "Ahhh, Chachi American break ultra jet crash mobile!" And then he kicks the sedan.

Two more Japanese punk rockers tumble out of the vehicle, laughing at the car accident. One has a shaved head and the other has big sideburns, a pompadour haircut, and sunglasses.

"No more jet mobile!" one of them says.

"Jet crash rock and roll!" the other says excitedly, then he howls like a wolf.

Tony opens the door and looks at them.

"Hey, he no Chachi American," the driver says.

"He like us," another says. "Rock and roll!"

They approach Tony.

"Normal American," the driver says, shooting bloody snot out of a nostril. "Are you part of the sick zip?"

Tony doesn't know what he's talking about.

"You wear Chachi clothes," he continues. "You drive Chachi no-jet car. You jet or you chachi?"

Tony has no idea what he's talking about. He pretends the Japanese punk rocker didn't ask him anything.

"I'm lost in this place," Tony says. "Are you lost too? Do you know a way out of this place? What is this place?"

The bloody-nosed punk frowns and puts on a pair of sunglasses. He widens his nostrils and pretends to be listening carefully to Tony's words.

"I've been driving around for days," Tony continues. "I'm trying to get out. My name is Tony, by the way."

Tony holds out his hand to see if the ultra fucker will shake it.

The punk looks at it. Then he leans his head back and says, "Hahahahah!"

The other punks also say, "Hahahahah!"

"He jet-Tony," the leader says, smiling. "He no Chachi-style."

"Hahahahah!" they say, while holding in their car crash wounds.

Then the leader rips off his sunglasses and says, "I Kawai Kazuki!"

"I Tom Nagata!" says the bald guy.

"I Izumi Headache!" says the pompadour hair.

Then, in perfect unison as if they have practiced this before, they say, "ULTRA JET LIFESTYLE!!! ROCK AND ROLL!!!"

Then they howl like wolves.

Tony smells gas. The SUV is leaking it into the street.

"Gas!" Tony says.

Kawai Kazuki looks at his pants. "Huh?" he says, looking at his shoes and his crotch. He doesn't understand.

Tony points at the gas and Kawai says something calmly in Japanese.

He snaps his fingers at his friends and they lift the collars on their leather jackets and follow him. Walking groovily away from the vehicles like they are trying to impress girls with their coolness, just in case there are girls watching for some reason. Tony begins to speed up, but Kawai grabs him by the elbow.

"No," Kawai says. "We only jet walk."

Tony wonders if the punks know how dangerous the situation is.

"We are always keep cool," says the ultra fucker. "You don't want to running. Only jet walk. We shall do to walking of new style."

The ultra fuckers jet walk away from the wreckage. Izumi Headache lights a cigarette and tosses the match behind him, which ignites the flame.

As the no-jet Chachi car and the ultra jet crash mobile explode behind them, the ultra fuckers never lose their cool. They stride slowly away from the fiery destruction, swigging bottles of vodka and smoking black death cigarettes.

Tom Nagata is the only one who turns to look at the

fire. "Hahahahah!" he says drunkenly at the flames, and howls like a wolf.

"What about the woman?" Tony asks.

"Huh?" Kawai says.

Whenever Kawai says *huh?* it reminds Tony of a drunken Japanese Scooby-Doo.

"There was a woman back there," he continues. "She had this weird mohawk and one of her eyes were missing."

"Huh? Crazy Chachi-woman?" he asks.

"She wasn't like the others," Tony says. "She smiled at me. She was different."

"Chachi woman big tits!" says Tom Nagata jumping between them, drunkenly slurring his words.

"No, I thought maybe you knew her," Tony says. "Have you heard anything about a cyclops?"

"Huh?" Kawai says. "Cyclops? Huh?"

"Where are we anyway?" Tony asks.

Kawai pulls on his bottom lip.

"What is this place?"

"Jet-Tony speaks too much Chachi!" Tom Nagata kids. "Jet-Tony likes the sick zip!"

"No," Kawai tells Nagata. "No, I see. Jet-Tony no know Chachi place."

Kawai turns to Tony. "This is crazy Japanese robot town."

"Robots?" Tony asks.

"Huh? Yeah, crazy Japanese robot town."

CHAPTER FIVE

CRAZY JAPANESE ROBOT TOWN

Tony is hanging out with the ultra fuckers in the Eagle Hills gated community; he is drinking large amounts of vodka and he is one hundred twenty-two hours and eleven minutes late for a dinner party.

He has difficulty communicating with these people. They only speak English, but their English isn't very good and they use a lot of slang that doesn't make sense to Tony. He doesn't know how they came to be trapped in this neighborhood or how long they have been here. But they do know many things about this place that Tony didn't know about. For instance, if you break open one of the walls in the dining room of any of the houses, there will be a liquor cabinet hidden away between the walls. It is full of Eagle Hills brand vodka and blue raspberry mixers.

The ultra fuckers have also shown him that every house has its own crawlspace in the attic, but you have to get to it from the backyard. Inside, there are a few dusty boxes containing some rather useful items. There are nails, a large hammer, a lighter, a gas can, a carton of cigarettes, a hunting knife, a sewing machine, thread, some paper plates, reading glasses, and cans of red, black, and white spray paint. The ultra fuckers are mostly just interested in the cigarettes, the paint, and the gas, but they also have a fondness for the knives and hammers.

Tony teaches them about the drive-thru restaurants. The ultra fuckers had tried to break into these buildings before but they said there wasn't anything in them. They weren't sure what they were for.

"Jet-Tony number one guy," Kawai said as Tony gave him a cheeseburger.

The ultra fuckers have had less luck finding food in the neighborhood. They had been forced to kill and eat the dogs and cats living in the homes in order to survive. They have been doing it for so long that they have grown used to it, but they are very grateful to Tony for giving them burgers and fries. He will feed them at the pop food drive-thrus until the balance on his debit card runs out, which will probably be in a few days.

Besides scavenging for supplies, the ultra fuckers enjoy getting extremely drunk and rampaging through the community, destroying the hideous uniformity, bringing chaos to order. Tony can appreciate their passion for wrecking the monotonous neighborhood, but it disturbs him when they decide to rape or kill the mundanes. They say the mundanes (or the chachi Americans, as they call them) are not real, they are only robots. The ultra fuckers don't feel bad about killing or raping robots.

But they look like real people. They bleed like real people.

"Just because they don't have the minds of real people doesn't mean it's okay to do what you want to them," Tony always says.

"Stay cool," is always their response. "Surf punk rock and roll."

Tony buys some new directions out of Eagle Hills. His old directions were burned when his car exploded after the crash. These directions take over where the last ones left off, but they seem to be longer than before.

The ultra fuckers agree to go with Tony. Well, he thinks they agreed. Kawai's response to his asking was "Huh? Leave sick zip all time? Rock and roll!" which sounded to him like a positive response.

They fill up an SUV with vodka bottles, hammers, paint cans, pillows, blankets, water jugs, cat jerky, and a whole lot of their stink, and head off down Pueblo Desert Ranch Lane. They let Tony drive so that they can get drunk. Tony kind of likes having company around, even though they tend to speak complete gibberish to him and often sit in their seats upside-down.

When they are hungry, they hit a drive-thru. When they need a bathroom, they break into a house. When Tony needs to sleep, he lets Kawai drive, hoping he doesn't get them lost.

It's going to take a long time before they reach the end of the list of directions, but Tony's not going to rest until he makes it to the exit.

After about forty hours of driving with the ultra fuckers, Tony's patience with them grows thin.

They lost all of their punk/noise cds when their last SUV exploded, so they try to compensate by recreating the songs themselves as loudly as they can. Izumi Headache sings the guitar sounds, Tom Nagata hits his knees like a drumset and sings the drumbeats with each strike, and Kawai Kazuki sings the lyrics. The songs were pure noise when originally recorded, but the all-vocal renditions of these songs are even noisier.

Tony comes to realize that the ultra fuckers were all in a band together before they arrived in Eagle Hills. It was probably a noisy punk band that he, nor anyone he knows, has ever heard about. Perhaps they were popular in Japan. He doesn't know. But they, particularly Izumi Headache, are giving him a major headache.

His headache is so bad that he almost doesn't see the woman stepping out in front of the SUV.

Tony hits the brakes just in time, tossing the upside-down sitters across the seats and plopping them onto their heads.

In front of the SUV, the cyclops girl is only a foot away form the bumper. She glances up at Tony, chewing on one of the bloody squirming goldfish that hangs down from the bangs of her fish-mohawk. She is Asian with large black eyes and red lipstick, wearing a black vinyl dress with a yellow belt and red shoulder pads. Her eye socket is leaking a florescent pink fluid. It seems like blood, but it is too bright and shiny.

Nagata pops his head up over the back seat, rubbing his head. "What happens?"

"Huh?" Kawai says as he sees the cyclops girl. "For real girl?"

The woman sucks down the goldfish. The goldfish on her mohawk click downward along a metal rod that curves around the arc of her skull. It brings a new goldfish one position forward, to fill the empty spot on her bangs. She smiles at them and winks.

Tony and the ultra fuckers watch her as she walks across the street and disappears around a corner.

"One-eye jet girl!" says Kawai Kazuki. "Go after her! Go! Go!"

"Uhhh," Tom Nagata groans at Kawai. "I don't like one-eye girls. They always so pokey."

"Huh?" Kawai says to Nagata. "Okay."

Tony goes after the girl, but she quickly drops out of sight. He finds himself on Sunset Pueblo Town Circle, which is a road that circles around a park identical to the park he had previously explored. The only difference between this park and the previous one is that there aren't any mundanes here.

"Where did she go?" Kawai asks.

He rolls down the window and sticks his spiky head outside.

"One eye girl!" he yells across the park. "I love fish mohawk! I love jet girl!"

But she isn't anywhere to be seen.

"Aww, she gone?" Kawai says. "Go find jet girl. Go."

Tony circles the park a couple times, but she is gone. He goes back to the road where they saw her and continues on their mission. No matter how much Kawai begs and complains, Tony doesn't go back to look for the cyclops. He doesn't want to get lost.

The car is really beginning to reek with the smell of four unshowered guys who haven't had access to deodorant for several days. Tony doesn't want to stop for anything now. They are on the last page of directions and he is sure that he will reach the destination before the end of the day.

"What you do when come out?" Kawai says. "Tom?"

"Uhhhh... " Tom Nagata says.

"I go crazy playstation video game," Izumi says.

Izumi imitates himself playing a crazy playstation video game by pretending to be fighting creatures with a laser samurai sword and he makes sound effects as he slashes.

"Uhhhh... " Nagata continues. "Oh! I fly remote plane!"

Nagata stretches his arms out like wings and makes loud airplane noises as he swoops from side to side in his seat. Kawai and Izumi push him when he swoops too close.

"Plane! Plane!" Kawai says. "Nevermind plane. I get gallon of beer and go surf punk live show!"

"Ohhh! Surf punk live show!" the others says, jealous they didn't think of it.

"With party and jet girls!" Izumi says.

"Though no one-eye girls," Nagata says, punching Izumi's shoulder.

"Jet-Tony. You?" asks Kawai.

It takes Tony a minute before he realizes they asked him a question. They watch him until he responds.

"I just want to go home," Tony says.

"Huh?" Kawai says. "Oh."

Like he's somehow disappointed.

Near twilight, they are only a couple turns away from their destination. They turn right on Navajo Canyon Creek Road and then left on Navajo Apache Pueblo Road and it should be right here somewhere.

"Keep an eye out for an exit," Tony says.

They drive down the road for a while, but there is no sign of an exit. Eventually, the street ends.

"Shit," he says.

He steps out of the car and screams, "Shit! Shit! Fuck you!"

The punks pile out of the car and jump up and down next to him screaming, "Shitty fuckers! Ultra fuck you!"

They don't seem to know why Tony is angry, but they

like to curse at things given the opportunity.

"Shitters!" Kawai says. "Piss biting ass packers!"

"Ultra fucking you all night!" Izumi says.

Tom Nagata gets a little carried away, jumping on the hood of the SUV and waving his fists at the sky.

"Take head, break!" he says. "Punch face bloody! Ultra fuckers on crack! Ultra fuck you!"

Tony hears something. He snaps his fingers at Kawai.

"Listen," Tony says.

Izumi stops screaming. The three of them can hear noises in the distance, but they can't hear them clearly over Nagata's screams.

"You die!" Nagata says. "Go die! Head on stick in air! Rock and roll!"

"Tom!" Kawai screams. "Get down from there. Quiet."

They listen.

In the distance, they hear hammering, sawing, and drilling.

They drive slowly through the streets, following the noise. At the top of a hill, they can see it all. Tony parks the car and gets out. He climbs onto the top of the SUV to get a better look.

At first, he's not quite sure what he's looking at. But then it hits him. It is the outskirts of the Eagle Hills gated community.

"It's growing," Tony says.

The edge of the neighborhood is like a tidal wave of destruction and creation. A row of bulldozers, rock-grinders, and a huge assortment of other strange machinery stretch as far as the eye can see in either direction. They are tearing down every tree, every car, every house, every mountain in their path, razing everything down into a smooth flat surface. Behind the demolishing machines, there are recycling machines that grind down all of the remains of the landscape and mold them into new materials. These new materials are then used to construct new houses, new cars, and new streets identical to all of the others in Eagle Hills.

Tony and the ultra fuckers haven't been able to get out of this place because it has been growing. It is taking over the landscape, taking over the countryside.

Outside of Eagle Hills, in the distance, Tony sees a foresty mountain town as it is getting demolished. He isn't even in Arizona anymore. He is in Colorado, or Montana, or even Canada. This one horrendous tract housing development is taking over the entire country.

He examines the construction equipment. There doesn't seem to be anyone running the machines. The houses seem to be building themselves. There isn't anyone controlling this. It is all automated.

Eagle Hills is building itself.

CHAPTER SIX

ONE-EYE JET GIRL, ROCK AND ROLL

For several days, Tony has been following the tidal wave of destruction and creation at the edge of the Eagle Hills gated community; he is running low on gas and he is three weeks two days four hours and fifty-three minutes late for a dinner party.

Past the outskirts of the community, Tony doesn't see land anymore. They are now over the Atlantic Ocean. The machines are dehydrating the ocean and transforming the land beneath into more tract housing.

"What do we do?" Tony asks the ultra fuckers.

"No more drive," Kawai says. "It all shit."

"All Chachi shit now," Nagata says.

Tony keeps driving until the gas runs out.

Out of gas on the side of a road, they just sit there staring out of the windows. Tony closes his eyes and tries to sleep.

"Whaa?" Izumi says.

Tony opens his eyes and turns around. Izumi is pointing at something in the street.

They all look to see the cyclops girl walking down the road toward them.

"Rock and roll!" Kawai screams. "Love is here!"

They all get out of the car. The woman walks up to

Tony, her fish mohawk flapping with her steps.

"Whoa, outerspace!" Kawai says to her.

"Come with me," she says.

They follow her down the road to one of the neighborhood parks. Kawai jet-walks next to her, checking her out.

"I love fish mohawk girl," he tells her.

She curls half a smile at him.

Once they get to the playground, the woman looks at Tony.

"Follow," she says.

Then she steps onto the merry-go-round.

Kawai follows her. Then Izumi and Nagata. As soon as Tony gets on, the woman opens a panel on one of the handlebars and flips a switch. The merry-go-round begins to descend into the earth.

Beneath the ground, there is another world. It is as large as a mall or an airport terminal.

"What is this place?" Tony asks.

"The control center of this quadrant," the woman says. "There is one of these in every quadrant. Each is operated by one of me."

"One of you?" Kawai says. "There more of you?"

"I have many duplicates," she says, smiling. "But we share the same consciousness. In a way, we are just one. But we can be in many, many places at the same time."

"What are you?" Tony asks.

"It is not important to know exactly what I am," she says. "I am not supposed to be here, just as none of you are supposed to be here. The best way to describe what I am to you is to compare myself to a computer virus. I am not a part of the plan. They are duplicating me by mistake."

She takes them into the control center.

"You are just robot?" Izumi asks.

"No," she says. "I am a programmed entity in flesh. I am like the other manufactured flesh entities in the houses above, only I evolved out of my original programming. I have a consciousness, awareness, emotions, intelligence. I am complex like you."

"What exactly caused all of this?" Tony asks. "Why is it happening?"

"It's a terraforming project that evolved from its original programming," she says. "It has developed its own awareness and intelligence, like myself. It's only goal is to restructure the environment to match its encoded configuration."

She flops her fish mohawk over her shoulder.

"Come look," she says.

She turns on a monitor. There is a section of the Eagle Hills housing development.

"This is a live video feed taken from satellite," she says.

"It is just one quadrant. There are four food dispensers, a park, and twenty blocks of houses per quadrant."

She zooms out to show the quadrant is surrounded by quadrants. She continues zooming out to show that there are hundreds of quadrants, thousands of quadrants, millions of quadrants. Then, once she's zoomed out all the way, they see that the entire Earth has been coated with them. The entire planet is just one enormous gated community.

The woman rotates the planet to show the back side, and then zooms in to a tiny speck of blue in the Atlantic Ocean.

"This is all that remains of the natural planet," she says.

They watch as the last of the natural world is swallowed up by tract housing.

"That's it?" Tony asks. "It's all gone?"

"It has all become restructured," she says.

"What about all the people?" he asks.

"All carbon-based matter has been broken down on a molecular level and reprocessed into foodstuffs or one of the flesh units, such as the mother unit, the father unit, the son unit, the daughter unit, the infant unit, the dog unit, the cat unit, the fish unit, or one of me."

Tony needs to take a seat.

"They're all dead?" he asks. "We're the only ones who haven't been processed into a part of the neighborhood?"

"No," she says. "There are many others like you. Several people found their way in through the front gates of the community. Perhaps a thousand people remain unprocessed."

"My units have been monitoring the other survivors," she says. "Not many of them have protested to the transformation as you have. Most of them have accepted their new way of life and seem to have made themselves at home. Some have had mental breakdowns and their minds force them to believe that they have always lived in the neighborhood. Others believe they have died and gone to Heaven. A few believe they have died and gone to Hell."

"Is my wife still alive?" Tony asks.

"Yes," the woman says. "Unfortunately, she is one of those that have suffered a severe mental breakdown. As we speak, she believes that she is a guest at a dinner party with her boss and his wife and children. She doesn't wonder why the party has lasted so many days."

"Where is she?" Tony asks. "I've got to find her. Can you give me directions to where she is?"

"Unfortunately," she says. "She will not live long enough for you to see her again."

"Why?" Tony asks. "Is she not able to take care of herself? Is she dying of hunger or thirst and doesn't even realize it?"

"No," says the woman. "She will likely be reprocessed during the second wave. After the last of the planet has been restructured, the neighborhood will start over again. It will tear itself down and restructure it as it did before. Everyone who survived the first wave will surely die in the second."

"We're die anyway?" Izumi asks.

"Not you," she says. "You're safe with me. That is why I brought you down here. I want to keep you all intact."

"What about the other survivors?" Tony asks.

"I have saved some of them in other quadrants," she says. "But as I said most of the people have adjusted to their lives in the community. They are lost in delusion and won't let me rescue them. Some have violently opposed my reasoning."

"There's got to be something you can do to stop this from happening?" Tony asks.

"I'm sorry. All I can do is save you. I have adequate supplies to keep you living, but there's no way to stop the housing development. There's no way to save any more people than I have already found."

"There's got to be a way," Tony says.

She shakes her head and eats a goldfish at him.

Tony, Tom Nagata, and Izumi Headache are sitting in plastic chairs, stewing in anger.

Kawai Kazuki is flirting with the cyclops girl and, surprisingly, she is flirting back. Perhaps she really does have the emotions she says she has or perhaps she has programmed responses to certain situations that appear to be emotions.

"Huh?" Kawai says to the girl as he lifts one of the fish

on her mohawk straight up in the air. It squirms out of his hand, plops against her forehead, and she giggles at him. "Hahahahah!" he says. "Fish mohawk! Outerspace hairstyle!"

Izumi Headache frowns at their leader.

"I don't want all our hard work go reset," Izumi says.

"Yeah," Tom Nagata says. "We work real hard making sick zip town into ultra jet lifestyle."

"Even if we redo it just change back later," Izumi says.

"Fucking shitters!" Nagata says.

"What think you do, jet-Tony?" Izumi says.

"There's got to be a way to stop it," Tony says. "There's always a way."

They nod their heads at him.

Two things Tony never wanted for his life were to give up hope or believe anyone who told him that something couldn't be done.

Izumi and Nagata have a talk with Kawai.

The cyclops girl is sitting in his lap and giggling until she hears what they have to say. The cyclops girl shakes Kawai's head for him. They argue in Japanese for awhile. Tony doesn't know what they are saying, but he can tell that Kawai refuses to help.

Izumi and Nagata push Kawai and flip him off. They leave the room and take Tony with them, cursing in English and Japanese at the same time.

CHAPTER SEVEN

MOSH HARD, LIFE CHEAP

Tony goes above ground as soon as the second wave of the Eagle Hills gated community passes over head; he is ready to cause some serious damage and he is really fucking late for a dinner party.

Tom Nagata and Izumi Headache are by his side. They have formulated a plan of attack and pray to whatever god hasn't been terraformed into part of a tract housing community that it works.

They charge across the park in three separate directions, heading for the nearest houses they can find. Each of them steal their own SUV and drive full speed toward the deconstruction/construction zone.

"Ultra fucker lifestyle!" Nagata screams out of his window at Tony.

Tony says, "Ultra fuck them dead!"

Nagata gives Tony a thumbs up for that.

Tony's plan is simple: they are just going to smash the hell out of all the construction equipment.

Nagata and Izumi scream one of their band's songs out of their SUV windows. They just sing the drum part and the guitar part, but they don't have Kawai with them to sing the vocals.

Once they close in on the outskirts of the second wave

of construction, the three suburban warriors scream their lungs out as they charge into battle.

"Let's do it!" Izumi screeches.

The three SUVs drive through half-built houses. They separate so that they don't accidentally hit each other. The SUVs crash through piles of wood and other materials. They break down the wooden skeletons of houses just beginning to be constructed.

Tony gets to the front line first and rams one of the recycling machines in front of one of the grinding machines. The grinding machine chews it into metal shreds and excretes it to be recycled, but it can't recycle itself. Once the constructing machines come forward, they are not sure what to do with the unprocessed remains but they attempt to build a house out of it anyway.

"It works!" Tony cries out. "We can damage it!"

Izumi Headache immediately understands what he has to do. He drives parallel with the edge of the wave and smashes into machine after machine with the side of his SUV. Almost every recycling machine he hits either tumbles into the blades of the demolishing machines or spins around and faces the wrong way, attempting to recycle the materials it has already processed.

The machinery doesn't know how to deal with chaos they are causing. It freezes up or turns in on itself. It wasn't prepared to get fucked by ultra fuckers.

Izumi's SUV slams into as much equipment as it can until it breaks apart and the engine is crushed. He doesn't give up, though. He leaps out of the vehicle and screams "Ultra fuck you!" then climbs up the back of a demolition machine. He gets a hold of the controls and hits switches and pulls levers until he figures out how it works. He rotates the demolition machine to the right and begins attacking the other demolition machines, grinding them up into scraps to be recycled.

Tony uses Izumi's tactic of slamming as many recycling machines as possible into the grinding machines. Soon, they realize that they have stopped a large section of the wave in its tracks. It can no longer terraform the neighborhood for a good two hundred feet. If only they would have done this during the first wave...

"Nagata! No!" Izumi says from atop the demolition machine as his friend comes barreling down the hill toward him.

Tom Nagata had wrecked his first SUV inside of one of the half-constructed homes and had to steal another. Now late in the game, Nagata doesn't know what is going on. He doesn't realize that his friend is driving the machine he wants to destroy.

"ROCK AND ROLL!" Nagata says as he smashes into the side of Izumi's demolition machine.

Izumi tumbles out and hits the ground, as his machine rolls around to the front of another demolition machine and they chew each other into pieces until neither of them work.

The crash shattered much of Nagata's SUV. He sits there rubbing his swollen forehead as a recycling machine grabs hold of his vehicle and begins to reshape it into housing material.

"ULTRA PUNK LIFESTYLE ROCK AND ROLL!!!" Nagata says from within the damaged vehicle as it gets recycled.

"Nagata!" Izumi cries, but he has to get to his feet and run away because he is in danger of becoming recycled himself.

Tony takes a look around. They have done considerable damage to the second wave of terraforming. So much, in fact, that the intelligence behind the terraforming program is forced to take action against them.

The manufactured flesh units are called into action. From the nearby houses, an army of mundane family members take to the streets and come after the ultra fuckers with hammers and knives.

Izumi screeches and runs away from them.

"Go die!" he screams at the mundanes. "Die now!"

Tony slams on the gas to go save him, but the SUV doesn't move. The engine is either broken or flooded. He has to abandon his vehicle. Mundane men and women come at him as soon as he jumps onto the ground. He rolls away and dodges their mechanical strikes. Kicking a mother in the stomach and pushing a son over to get onto his feet.

Hammers clang against the machines next to him as he runs. Mundane fathers are throwing them like axes, aiming for his head. He climbs up the back of one of the demolition machines, and feels a butcher knife stabbing through the bottom of his foot as one of the daughter clones sneaks up beneath him.

Tony cries out. He pulls his foot off the blade and continues climbing. A thrown hammer hits him on the back of the shoulder. Another hits him on the lower spine. But he makes it to the top of the machine and seizes the controls. Before another hammer can be tossed at him, he turns the deconstruction vehicle on the mundanes.

"Ultra fuck you!" Tony screams in a fake Japanese accent, plowing into the crowd of cookie-cutter zombies and chewing them into tiny bits of meat.

Another SUV comes roaring over the hill. It slams through the horde of dad, mom, and kid clones, destroying everything in its path.

"Ultra jet fuckers!" Kawai Kazuki screams through the window as he pulls up alongside Izumi, who has so many hammer-bruises on him that he looks like a Dalmatian.

The cyclops girl opens the door and helps Izumi in. Then they speed off toward Tony.

"The brain!" Kawai tells Tony. "Kill the brain!"

But Tony can't hear him over the crushing and grinding of mundane flesh and bones.

The cyclops girl jumps out of the SUV and charges toward Tony's vehicle.

"Attack the memory banks!" she calls up to him, pointing toward a large round vehicle at the heart of the demolition machines.

He hears her and gives her a thumbs up.

She winks her one eye and smiles up at him. Then she is chewed into pieces by the blades of a grinding machine.

"Jet girl, noooo!" Kawai cries.

The mundanes have taken control of the demolition vehicles and are turning them on the ultra fuckers. Kawai turns the wheel just in time to avoid grinder blades from biting into the side of the SUV.

Two more grinder machines come after Tony. They know he is going after the nerve center. He slams into the side of one grinder that is blocking his way to the brain. A mundane drives the teeth of his machine into Tony's rear and he is forced to leap out onto the ground.

Dodging grinder blades and mundanes with knives, Tony makes it to the back of the brain vehicle.

"Now what?" he says.

He doesn't really have anything to break it with.

He tries hitting the vehicle with a hammer, but it is made of strong stuff. The blades of a grinding machine are heading toward him, chopping up other mundanes as it goes.

Tony leaps out of the way as he sees Kawai's SUV charging at the rear of the mundane's grinder. He slams full speed into the vehicle and the grinder is propelled forward into the central brain of the Eagle Hills construction system.

It chews right through to the other side.

Destroying the brain didn't do exactly what Tony expected it to do. The mundanes are no longer attacking. They just stare at each other with librarian faces. But the machines keep going. They are making some funny noises, but they keep on destructing and constructing.

Tony drops to the ground. He doesn't know what else to do.

Kawai Kazuki steps out of the SUV and approaches the dead brain. Izumi Headache stumbles into the dirt behind him.

Kawai just sighs and watches as the machines continue on.

"Thanks," Tony says.

"I miss one-eye jet girl," he says.

Without the brain, the machines eventually stop working, but not before terraforming several miles of the neighborhood. However, without the computer, the terraforming didn't go according to plan. These quadrants of housing are strange and chaotic. There are streets made of yellow summer dresses, mothers with fish heads, houses with pop food for walls, daughters with gravel skin, dogs with hammer legs, and a hundred other random variations that defy all logic and order.

Tom Nagata appears behind the wounded Izumi.

"Ultra jet town," Nagata says about the new neighborhood.

Izumi turns around and sees his friend still alive.

"Nagata!" he cries with laughter and hugs him, lifting him up into the air.

Izumi notices something different about his friend.

"Hey, outerspace leg-style!" Izumi says.

He points at Nagata's legs, which have been recycled into SUV wheels.

"Whaa?" Nagata says, as if he didn't notice anything wrong about them. He looks down and cries, "OH!" Then he says "Hahahahah!" and hops on his wheel-legs from side to side.

Kawai mopes away from his friends. He takes off his sunglasses and frowns at the tract housing behind him.

"Hey, jet boy," the cyclops girl calls out, running down the hill toward him.

"Huh?" Kawai says, looking up at her.

"One-eye outerspace girl!" he cries.

She wraps her arms around him and kisses his neck. Her goldfish mohawk tickles his ear. Another copy of the cyclops girl approaches him from behind and hugs him around the waist.

"Huh?" Kawai says.

"Oh!" he says, and hugs them both. "Hahahahah!"

He can have as many outerspace cyclops girls as he wants.

The ultra fuckers have succeeded in creating a world of beautiful chaos. They say goodbye to their new friend, Tony. They give him high-fives and pat him on the back.

Then all four of them say "ULTRA JET LIFESTYLE!!!" in unison, as if they have practiced it before.

And Tony says, "Rock and roll!"

"Hahahahah!" Kawai says.

The three Japanese punks and the cyclops girls enter the surreal version of the Eagle Hills gated community and begin to search for a new home.

CHAPTER EIGHT

LIFE IS ONLY KILLING TIME BETWEEN MASTURBATIONS

Two things Tony never wanted for his life were to blindly lead a mundane existence or ever be separated from the woman he loved most in the world.

One of the cyclops girls gave him directions to the house Tammy is staying at. The directions might be fifty pages long, but he will get there as soon as he can. And once he does, he will help bring her back to reality and build a completely new life with her.

Tony is traveling all alone through the streets of the Eagle Hills gated community; he is wearing a fresh new smile on his face and he is three weeks five days ten hours and thirty-one minutes late for a dinner party.

ABOUT THE AUTHOR

Carlton Mellick III is one of the leading authors of the bizarro fiction subgenre. Since 2001, his books have drawn an international cult following, despite the fact that they have been shunned by most libraries and chain bookstores.

He won the Wonderland Book Award for his novel, *Warrior Wolf Women of the Wasteland*, in 2009. His short fiction has appeared in *Vice Magazine, The Year's Best Fantasy and Horror #16, The Magazine of Bizarro Fiction,* and *Zombies: Encounters with the Hungry Dead*, among others. He is also a graduate of Clarion West, where he studied under the likes of Chuck Palahniuk, Connie Willis, and Cory Doctorow.

He lives in Portland, OR, the bizarro fiction mecca.

Visit him online at **www.carltonmellick.com**

Bizarro Books

CATALOG   SPRING 2012

ERASERHEAD PRESS

Swallowdown
Press

LAZY FASCIST

Your major resource for the bizarro fiction genre:

WWW.BIZARROCENTRAL.COM

Introduce yourselves to the bizarro fiction genre and all of its authors with the Bizarro Starter Kit series. Each volume features short novels and short stories by ten of the leading bizarro authors, designed to give you a perfect sampling of the genre for only $10.

BB-0X1
"The Bizarro Starter Kit" (Orange)
Featuring D. Harlan Wilson, Carlton Mellick III, Jeremy Robert Johnson, Kevin L Donihe, Gina Ranalli, Andre Duza, Vincent W. Sakowski, Steve Beard, John Edward Lawson, and Bruce Taylor. **236 pages $10**

BB-0X2
"The Bizarro Starter Kit" (Blue)
Featuring Ray Fracalossy, Jeremy C. Shipp, Jordan Krall, Mykle Hansen, Andersen Prunty, Eckhard Gerdes, Bradley Sands, Steve Aylett, Christian TeBordo, and Tony Rauch. **244 pages $10**

BB-0X2
"The Bizarro Starter Kit" (Purple)
Featuring Russell Edson, Athena Villaverde, David Agranoff, Matthew Revert, Andrew Goldfarb, Jeff Burk, Garrett Cook, Kris Saknussemm, Cody Goodfellow, and Cameron Pierce **264 pages $10**

BB-001 **"The Kafka Effekt" D. Harlan Wilson** — A collection of forty-four irreal short stories loosely written in the vein of Franz Kafka, with more than a pinch of William S. Burroughs sprinkled on top. **211 pages $14**

BB-002 **"Satan Burger" Carlton Mellick III** — The cult novel that put Carlton Mellick III on the map ... Six punks get jobs at a fast food restaurant owned by the devil in a city violently overpopulated by surreal alien cultures. **236 pages $14**

BB-003 **"Some Things Are Better Left Unplugged" Vincent Sakwoski** — Join The Man and his Nemesis, the obese tabby, for a nightmare roller coaster ride into this postmodern fantasy. **152 pages $10**

BB-004 **"Shall We Gather At the Garden?" Kevin L Donihe** — Donihe's Debut novel. Midgets take over the world, The Church of Lionel Richie vs. The Church of the Byrds, plant porn and more! **244 pages $14**

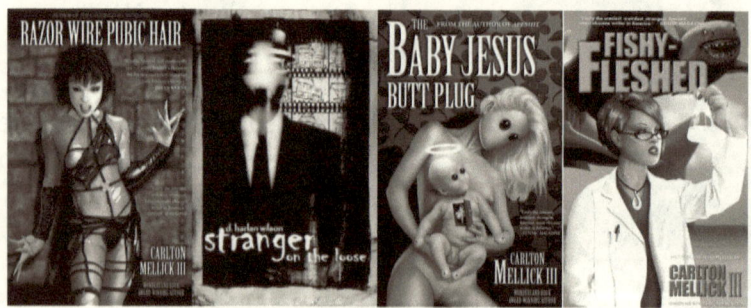

BB-005 **"Razor Wire Pubic Hair" Carlton Mellick III** — A genderless humandildo is purchased by a razor dominatrix and brought into her nightmarish world of bizarre sex and mutilation. **176 pages $11**

BB-006 **"Stranger on the Loose" D. Harlan Wilson** — The fiction of Wilson's 2nd collection is planted in the soil of normalcy, but what grows out of that soil is a dark, witty, otherworldly jungle... **228 pages $14**

BB-007 **"The Baby Jesus Butt Plug" Carlton Mellick III** — Using clones of the Baby Jesus for anal sex will be the hip sex fetish of the future. **92 pages $10**

BB-008 **"Fishyfleshed" Carlton Mellick III** — The world of the past is an illogical flatland lacking in dimension and color, a sick-scape of crispy squid people wandering the desert for no apparent reason. **260 pages $14**

BB-009 **"Dead Bitch Army" Andre Duza** — Step into a world filled with racist teenagers, cannibals, 100 warped Uncle Sams, automobiles with razor-sharp teeth, living graffiti, and a pissed-off zombie bitch out for revenge. **344 pages $16**

BB-010 **"The Menstruating Mall" Carlton Mellick III** — "The Breakfast Club meets Chopping Mall as directed by David Lynch." - Brian Keene **212 pages $12**

BB-011 **"Angel Dust Apocalypse" Jeremy Robert Johnson** — Meth-heads, man-made monsters, and murderous Neo-Nazis. "Seriously amazing short stories..." - Chuck Palahniuk, author of Fight Club **184 pages $11**

BB-012 **"Ocean of Lard" Kevin L Donihe / Carlton Mellick III** — A parody of those old Choose Your Own Adventure kid's books about some very odd pirates sailing on a sea made of animal fat. **176 pages $12**

BB-015 **"Foop!" Chris Genoa** — Strange happenings are going on at Dactyl, Inc, the world's first and only time travel tourism company.
"A surreal pie in the face!" - Christopher Moore **300 pages $14**

BB-020 **"Punk Land" Carlton Mellick III** — In the punk version of Heaven, the anarchist utopia is threatened by corporate fascism and only Goblin, Mortician's sperm, and a blue-mohawked female assassin named Shark Girl can stop them. **284 pages $15**

BB-027 **"Siren Promised" Jeremy Robert Johnson & Alan M Clark** — Nominated for the Bram Stoker Award. A potent mix of bad drugs, bad dreams, brutal bad guys, and surreal/incredible art by Alan M. Clark. **190 pages $13**

BB-031 **"Sea of the Patchwork Cats" Carlton Mellick III** — A quiet dreamlike tale set in the ashes of the human race. For Mellick enthusiasts who also adore The Twilight Zone. **112 pages $10**

BB-032 **"Extinction Journals" Jeremy Robert Johnson** — An uncanny voyage across a newly nuclear America where one man must confront the problems associated with loneliness, insane dieties, radiation, love, and an ever-evolving cockroach suit with a mind of its own. **104 pages $10**

BB-037 **"The Haunted Vagina" Carlton Mellick III** — It's difficult to love a woman whose vagina is a gateway to the world of the dead. **132 pages $10**

BB-043 **"War Slut" Carlton Mellick III** — Part "1984," part "Waiting for Godot," and part action horror video game adaptation of John Carpenter's "The Thing." **116 pages $10**

BB-047 **"Sausagey Santa" Carlton Mellick III** — A bizarro Christmas tale featuring Santa as a piratey mutant with a body made of sausages. 124 pages $10

BB-048 **"Misadventures in a Thumbnail Universe" Vincent Sakowski** — Dive deep into the surreal and satirical realms of neo-classical Blender Fiction, filled with television shoes and flesh-filled skies. **120 pages $10**

BB-053 **"Ballad of a Slow Poisoner" Andrew Goldfarb** — Millford Mutterwurst sat down on a Tuesday to take his afternoon tea, and made the unpleasant discovery that his elbows were becoming flatter. **128 pages $10**

BB-055 **"Help! A Bear is Eating Me" Mykle Hansen** — The bizarro, heartwarming, magical tale of poor planning, hubris and severe blood loss... **150 pages $11**

BB-056 **"Piecemeal June" Jordan Krall** — A man falls in love with a living sex doll, but with love comes danger when her creator comes after her with crab-squid assassins. **90 pages $9**

BB-058 **"The Overwhelming Urge" Andersen Prunty** — A collection of bizarro tales by Andersen Prunty. **150 pages $11**

BB-059 **"Adolf in Wonderland" Carlton Mellick III** — A dreamlike adventure that takes a young descendant of Adolf Hitler's design and sends him down the rabbit hole into a world of imperfection and disorder. **180 pages $11**

BB-061 **"Ultra Fuckers" Carlton Mellick III** — Absurdist suburban horror about a couple who enter an upper middle class gated community but can't find their way out. **108 pages $9**

BB-062 **"House of Houses" Kevin L. Donihe** — An odd man wants to marry his house. Unfortunately, all of the houses in the world collapse at the same time in the Great House Holocaust. Now he must travel to House Heaven to find his departed fiancee. **172 pages $11**

BB-064 **"Squid Pulp Blues" Jordan Krall** — In these three bizarro-noir novellas, the reader is thrown into a world of murderers, drugs made from squid parts, deformed gun-toting veterans, and a mischievous apocalyptic donkey. **204 pages $12**

BB-065 **"Jack and Mr. Grin" Andersen Prunty** — "When Mr. Grin calls you can hear a smile in his voice. Not a warm and friendly smile, but the kind that seizes your spine in fear. You don't need to pay your phone bill to hear it. That smile is in every line of Prunty's prose." - Tom Bradley. **208 pages $12**

BB-066 **"Cybernetrix" Carlton Mellick III** — What would you do if your normal everyday world was slowly mutating into the video game world from Tron? **212 pages $12**

BB-072 **"Zerostrata" Andersen Prunty** — Hansel Nothing lives in a tree house, suffers from memory loss, has a very eccentric family, and falls in love with a woman who runs naked through the woods every night. **144 pages $11**

BB-073 "The Egg Man" Carlton Mellick III — It is a world where humans reproduce like insects. Children are the property of corporations, and having an enormous ten-foot brain implanted into your skull is a grotesque sexual fetish. Mellick's industrial urban dystopia is one of his darkest and grittiest to date. **184 pages $11**

BB-074 "Shark Hunting in Paradise Garden" Cameron Pierce — A group of strange humanoid religious fanatics travel back in time to the Garden of Eden to discover it is invested with hundreds of giant flying maneating sharks. **150 pages $10**

BB-075 "Apeshit" Carlton Mellick III - Friday the 13th meets Visitor Q. Six hipster teens go to a cabin in the woods inhabited by a deformed killer. An incredibly fucked-up parody of B-horror movies with a bizarro slant. **192 pages $12**

BB-076 "Fuckers of Everything on the Crazy Shitting Planet of the Vomit At smosphere" Mykle Hansen - Three bizarro satires. Monster Cocks, Journey to the Center of Agnes Cuddlebottom, and Crazy Shitting Planet. **228 pages $12**

BB-077 "The Kissing Bug" Daniel Scott Buck — In the tradition of Roald Dahl, Tim Burton, and Edward Gorey, comes this bizarro anti-war children's story about a bohemian conenose kissing bug who falls in love with a human woman. **116 pages $10**

BB-078 "MachoPoni" Lotus Rose — It's My Little Pony... *Bizarro* style! A long time ago Poniworld was split in two. On one side of the Jagged Line is the Pastel Kingdom, a magical land of music, parties, and positivity. On the other side of the Jagged Line is Dark Kingdom inhabited by an army of undead ponies. **148 pages $11**

BB-079 "The Faggiest Vampire" Carlton Mellick III — A Roald Dahl-esque children's story about two faggy vampires who partake in a mustache competition to find out which one is truly the faggiest. **104 pages $10**

BB-080 "Sky Tongues" Gina Ranalli — The autobiography of Sky Tongues, the biracial hermaphrodite actress with tongues for fingers. Follow her strange life story as she rises from freak to fame. **204 pages $12**

BB-081 "Washer Mouth" Kevin L. Donihe - A washing machine becomes human and pursues his dream of meeting his favorite soap opera star. **244 pages $11**

BB-082 "Shatnerquake" Jeff Burk - All of the characters ever played by William Shatner are suddenly sucked into our world. Their mission: hunt down and destroy the real William Shatner. **100 pages $10**

BB-083 "The Cannibals of Candyland" Carlton Mellick III - There exists a race of cannibals that are made of candy. They live in an underground world made out of candy. One man has dedicated his life to killing them all. **170 pages $11**

BB-084 "Slub Glub in the Weird World of the Weeping Willows" **Andrew Goldfarb -** The charming tale of a blue glob named Slub Glub who helps the weeping willows whose tears are flooding the earth. There are also hyenas, ghosts, and a voodoo priest **100 pages $10**

BB-085 "Super Fetus" Adam Pepper - Try to abort this fetus and he'll kick your ass! **104 pages $10**

BB-086 "Fistful of Feet" Jordan Krall - A bizarro tribute to spaghetti westerns, featuring Cthulhu-worshipping Indians, a woman with four feet, a crazed gunman who is obsessed with sucking on candy, Syphilis-ridden mutants, sexually transmitted tattoos, and a house devoted to the freakiest fetishes. **228 pages $12**

BB-087 "Ass Goblins of Auschwitz" Cameron Pierce - It's Monty Python meets Nazi exploitation in a surreal nightmare as can only be imagined by Bizarro author Cameron Pierce. **104 pages $10**

BB-088 "Silent Weapons for Quiet Wars" Cody Goodfellow - "This is high-end psychological surrealist horror meets bottom-feeding low-life crime in a techno-thrilling science fiction world full of Lovecraft and magic..." -John Skipp **212 pages $12**

BB-089 **"Warrior Wolf Women of the Wasteland"** **Carlton Mellick III**
— Road Warrior Werewolves versus McDonaldland Mutants...post-apocalyptic fiction has never been quite like this. **316 pages $13**

BB-091 **"Super Giant Monster Time"** **Jeff Burk** — A tribute to choose your own adventures and Godzilla movies. Will you escape the giant monsters that are rampaging the fuck out of your city and shit? Or will you join the mob of alien-controlled punk rockers causing chaos in the streets? What happens next depends on you. **188 pages $12**

BB-092 **"Perfect Union"** **Cody Goodfellow** — "Cronenberg's THE FLY on a grand scale: human/insect gene-spliced body horror, where the human hive politics are as shocking as the gore." -John Skipp. **272 pages $13**

BB-093 **"Sunset with a Beard"** **Carlton Mellick III** — 14 stories of surreal science fiction. **200 pages $12**

BB-094 **"My Fake War"** **Andersen Prunty** — The absurd tale of an unlikely soldier forced to fight a war that, quite possibly, does not exist. It's Rambo meets Waiting for Godot in this subversive satire of American values and the scope of the human imagination. **128 pages $11**

BB-095 **"Lost in Cat Brain Land"** **Cameron Pierce** — Sad stories from a surreal world. A fascist mustache, the ghost of Franz Kafka, a desert inside a dead cat. Primordial entities mourn the death of their child. The desperate serve tea to mysterious creatures. A hopeless romantic falls in love with a pterodactyl. And much more. **152 pages $11**

BB-096 **"The Kobold Wizard's Dildo of Enlightenment +2"** **Carlton Mellick III** — A Dungeons and Dragons parody about a group of people who learn they are only made up characters in an AD&D campaign and must find a way to resist their nerdy teenaged players and retarded dungeon master in order to survive. 232 **pages $12**

BB-098 **"A Hundred Horrible Sorrows of Ogner Stump"** **Andrew Goldfarb** — Goldfarb's acclaimed comic series. A magical and weird journey into the horrors of everyday life. **164 pages $11**

BB-099 "Pickled Apocalypse of Pancake Island" Cameron Pierce—A demented fairy tale about a pickle, a pancake, and the apocalypse. **102 pages $8**

BB-100 "Slag Attack" Andersen Prunty— Slag Attack features four visceral, noir stories about the living, crawling apocalypse.A slag is what survivors are calling the slug-like maggots raining from the sky, burrowing inside people, and hollowing out their flesh and their sanity. **148 pages $11**

BB-101 "Slaughterhouse High" Robert Devereaux—A place where schools are built with secret passageways, rebellious teens get zippers installed in their mouths and genitals, and once a year, on that special night, one couple is slaughtered and the bits of their bodies are kept as souvenirs. **304 pages $13**

BB-102 "The Emerald Burrito of Oz" John Skipp & Marc Levinthal —OZ IS REAL! Magic is real! The gate is really in Kansas! And America is finally allowing Earth tourists to visit this weird-ass, mysterious land. But when Gene of Los Angeles heads off for summer vacation in the Emerald City, little does he know that a war is brewing...a war that could destroy both worlds. **280 pages $13**

BB-103 "The Vegan Revolution... with Zombies" David Agranoff — When there's no more meat in hell, the vegans will walk the earth. **160 pages $11**

BB-104 "The Flappy Parts" Kevin L Donihe—Poems about bunnies, LSD, and police abuse. You know, things that matter. 132 **pages $11**

BB-105 "Sorry I Ruined Your Orgy" Bradley Sands—Bizarro humorist Bradley Sands returns with one of the strangest, most hilarious collections of the year. **130 pages $11**

BB-106 "Mr. Magic Realism" Bruce Taylor—Like Golden Age science fiction comics written by Freud, *Mr. Magic Realism* is a strange, insightful adventure that spans the furthest reaches of the galaxy, exploring the hidden caverns in the hearts and minds of men, women, aliens, and biomechanical cats. **152 pages $11**

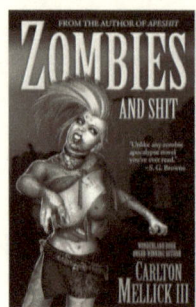

BB-107 "Zombies and Shit" Carlton Mellick III—"Battle Royale" meets "Return of the Living Dead." Mellick's bizarro tribute to the zombie genre. **308 pages $13**

BB-108 "The Cannibal's Guide to Ethical Living" Mykle Hansen—Over a five star French meal of fine wine, organic vegetables and human flesh, a lunatic delivers a witty, chilling, disturbingly sane argument in favor of eating the rich.. **184 pages $11**

BB-109 "Starfish Girl" Athena Villaverde—In a post-apocalyptic underwater dome society, a girl with a starfish growing from her head and an assassin with sea anenome hair are on the run from a gang of mutant fish men. **160 pages $11**

BB-110 "Lick Your Neighbor" Chris Genoa—Mutant ninjas, a talking whale, kung fu masters, maniacal pilgrims, and an alcoholic clown populate Chris Genoa's surreal, darkly comical and unnerving reimagining of the first Thanksgiving. **303 pages $13**

BB-111 "Night of the Assholes" Kevin L. Donihe—A plague of assholes is infecting the countryside. Normal everyday people are transforming into jerks, snobs, dicks, and douchebags. And they all have only one purpose: to make your life a living hell.. **192 pages $11**

BB-112 "Jimmy Plush, Teddy Bear Detective" Garrett Cook—Hardboiled cases of a private detective trapped within a teddy bear body. **180 pages $11**

BB-113 "The Deadheart Shelters" Forrest Armstrong—The hip hop lovechild of William Burroughs and Dali... **144 pages $11**

BB-114 "Eyeballs Growing All Over Me... Again" Tony Raugh—Absurd, surreal, playful, dream-like, whimsical, and a lot of fun to read. **144 pages $11**

BB-115 "Whargoul" Dave Brockie — From the killing grounds of Stalingrad to the death camps of the holocaust. From torture chambers in Iraq to race riots in the United States, the Whargoul was there, killing and raping. **244 pages $12**

BB-116 "By the Time We Leave Here, We'll Be Friends" J. David Osborne — A David Lynchian nightmare set in a Russian gulag, where its prisoners, guards, traitors, soldiers, lovers, and demons fight for survival and their own rapidly deteriorating humanity. **168 pages $11**

BB-117 "Christmas on Crack" edited by Carlton Mellick III — Perverted Christmas Tales for the whole family! . . . as long as every member of your family is over the age of 18. **168 pages $11**

BB-118 "Crab Town" Carlton Mellick III — Radiation fetishists, balloon people, mutant crabs, sail-bike road warriors, and a love affair between a woman and an H-Bomb. This is one mean asshole of a city. Welcome to Crab Town. **100 pages $8**

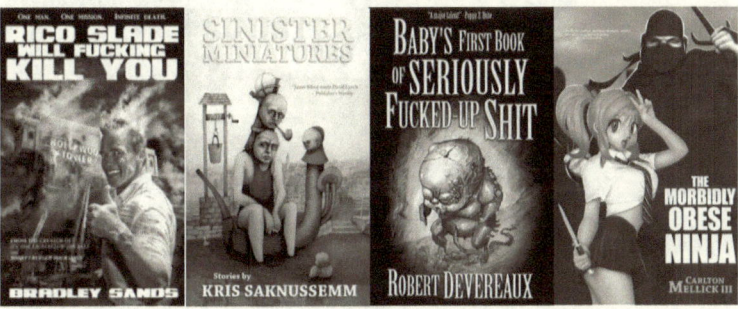

BB-119 "Rico Slade Will Fucking Kill You" Bradley Sands — Rico Slade is an action hero. Rico Slade can rip out a throat with his bare hands. Rico Slade's favorite food is the honey-roasted peanut. Rico Slade will fucking kill everyone. A novel. **122 pages $8**

BB-120 "Sinister Miniatures" Kris Saknussemm — The definitive collection of short fiction by Kris Saknussemm, confirming that he is one of the best, most daring writers of the weird to emerge in the twenty-first century. **180 pages $11**

BB-121 "Baby's First Book of Seriously Fucked up Shit" Robert Devereaux — Ten stories of the strange, the gross, and the just plain fucked up from one of the most original voices in horror. **176 pages $11**

BB-122 "The Morbidly Obese Ninja" Carlton Mellick III — These days, if you want to run a successful company . . . you're going to need a lot of ninjas. **92 pages $8**

BB-123 **"Abortion Arcade" Cameron Pierce** — An intoxicating blend of body horror and midnight movie madness, reminiscent of early David Lynch and the splatterpunks at their most sublime. **172 pages $11**

BB-124 **"Black Hole Blues" Patrick Wensink** — A hilarious double helix of country music and physics. **196 pages $11**

BB-125 **"Barbarian Beast Bitches of the Badlands" Carlton Mellick III** — Three prequels and sequels to *Warrior Wolf Women of the Wasteland*. **284 pages $13**

BB-126 **"The Traveling Dildo Salesman" Kevin L. Donihe** — A nightmare comedy about destiny, faith, and sex toys. Also featuring Donihe's most lurid and infamous short stories: *Milky Agitation, Two-Way Santa, The Helen Mower, Living Room Zombies,* and *Revenge of the Living Masturbation Rag*. **108 pages $8**

BB-127 **"Metamorphosis Blues" Bruce Taylor** — Enter a land of love beasts, intergalactic cowboys, and rock 'n roll. A land where Sears Catalogs are doorways to insanity and men keep mysterious black boxes. Welcome to the monstrous mind of Mr. Magic Realism. **136 pages $11**

BB-128 **"The Driver's Guide to Hitting Pedestrians" Andersen Prunty** — A pocket guide to the twenty-three most painful things in life, written by the most well-adjusted man in the universe. **108 pages $8**

BB-129 **"Island of the Super People" Kevin Shamel** — Four students and their anthropology professor journey to a remote island to study its indigenous population. But this is no ordinary native culture. They're super heroes and villains with flesh costumes and out-landish abilities like self-detonation, musical eyelashes, and microwave hands. **194 pages $11**

BB-130 **"Fantastic Orgy" Carlton Mellick III** — Shark Sex, mutant cats, and strange sexually transmitted diseases. Featuring the stories: *Candy-coated, Ear Cat, Fantastic Orgy, City Hobgoblins,* and *Porno in August*. **136 pages $9**

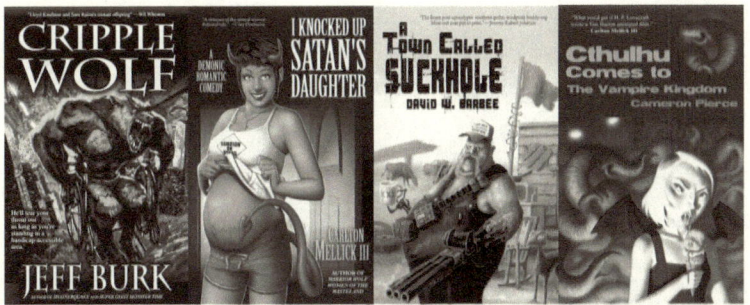

BB-131 "Cripple Wolf" Jeff Burk — Part man. Part wolf. 100% crippled. Also including *Punk Rock Nursing Home*, *Adrift with Space Badgers*, *Cook for Your Life*, *Just Another Day in the Park*, *Frosty and the Full Monty*, and *House of Cats*. **152 pages $10**

BB-132 "I Knocked Up Satan's Daughter" Carlton Mellick III — An adorable, violent, fantastical love story. A romantic comedy for the bizarro fiction reader. **152 pages $10**

BB-133 "A Town Called Suckhole" David W. Barbee — Far into the future, in the nuclear bowels of post-apocalyptic Dixie, there is a town. A town of derelict mobile homes, ancient junk, and mutant wildlife. A town of slack jawed rednecks who bask in the splendors of moonshine and mud boggin'. A town dedicated to the bloody and demented legacy of the Old South. A town called Suckhole. **144 pages $10**

BB-134 "Cthulhu Comes to the Vampire Kingdom" Cameron Pierce — What you'd get if H. P. Lovecraft wrote a Tim Burton animated film. **148 pages $11**

BB-135 "I am Genghis Cum" Violet LeVoit — From the savage Arctic tundra to post-partum mutations to your missing daughter's unmarked grave, join visionary madwoman Violet LeVoit in this non-stop eight-story onslaught of full-tilt Bizarro punk lit thrills. **124 pages $9**

BB-136 "Haunt" Laura Lee Bahr — A tripping-balls Los Angeles noir, where a mysterious dame drags you through a time-warping Bizarro hall of mirrors. **316 pages $13**

BB-137 "Amazing Stories of the Flying Spaghetti Monster" edited by Cameron Pierce — Like an all-spaghetti evening of Adult Swim, the Flying Spaghetti Monster will show you the many realms of His Noodly Appendage. Learn of those who worship him and the lives he touches in distant, mysterious ways. **228 pages $12**

BB-138 "Wave of Mutilation" Douglas Lain — A dream-pop exploration of modern architecture and the American identity, *Wave of Mutilation* is a Zen finger trap for the 21st century. **100 pages $8**

BB-139 **"Hooray for Death!" Mykle Hansen** — Famous Author Mykle Hansen draws unconventional humor from deaths tiny and large, and invites you to laugh while you can. **128 pages $10**

BB-140 **"Hypno-hog's Moonshine Monster Jamboree" Andrew Goldfarb** — Hicks, Hogs, Horror! Goldfarb is back with another strange illustrated tale of backwoods weirdness. **120 pages $9**

BB-141 **"Broken Piano For President" Patrick Wensink** — A comic masterpiece about the fast food industry, booze, and the necessity to choose happiness over work and security. **372 pages $15**

BB-142 **"Please Do Not Shoot Me in the Face" Bradley Sands** — A novel in three parts, *Please Do Not Shoot Me in the Face: A Novel*, is the story of one boy detective, the worst ninja in the world, and the great American fast food wars. It is a novel of loss, destruction, and--incredibly--genuine hope. **224 pages $12**

BB-143 **"Santa Steps Out" Robert Devereaux** — Sex, Death, and Santa Claus ... The ultimate erotic Christmas story is back. **294 pages $13**

BB-144 **"Santa Conquers the Homophobes" Robert Devereaux** — "I wish I could hope to ever attain one-thousandth the perversity of Robert Devereaux's toenail clippings." - Poppy Z. Brite **316 pages $13**

BB-145 **"We Live Inside You" Jeremy Robert Johnson** — "Jeremy Robert Johnson is dancing to a way different drummer. He loves language, he loves the edge, and he loves us people. These stories have range and style and wit. This is entertainment... and literature."- Jack Ketchum **188 pages $11**

BB-146 **"Clockwork Girl" Athena Villaverde** — Urban fairy tales for the weird girl in all of us. Like a combination of Francesca Lia Block, Charles de Lint, Kathe Koja, Tim Burton, and Hayao Miyazaki, her stories are cute, kinky, edgy, magical, provocative, and strange, full of poetic imagery and vicious sexuality. **160 pages $10**

BB-147 **"Armadillo Fists" Carlton Mellick III** — A weird-as-hell gangster story set in a world where people drive giant mechanical dinosaurs instead of cars. **168 pages $11**

BB-148 **"Gargoyle Girls of Spider Island" Cameron Pierce** — Four college seniors venture out into open waters for the tropical party weekend of a lifetime. Instead of a teenage sex fantasy, they find themselves in a nightmare of pirates, sharks, and sex-crazed monsters. **100 pages $8**

BB-149 **"The Handsome Squirm" by Carlton Mellick III** — Like Franz Kafka's *The Trial* meets an erotic body horror version of *The Blob*. **158 pages $11**

BB-150 **"Tentacle Death Trip" Jordan Krall** — It's *Death Race 2000* meets H. P. Lovecraft in bizarro author Jordan Krall's best and most suspenseful work to date. **224 pages $12**

BB-151 **"The Obese" Nick Antosca** — Like Alfred Hitchcock's *The Birds*... but with obese people. **108 pages $10**

BB-152 **"All-Monster Action!" Cody Goodfellow** — The world gave him a blank check and a demand: Create giant monsters to fight our wars. But Dr. Otaku was not satisfied with mere chaos and mass destruction.... **216 pages $12**

BB-153 **"Ugly Heaven" Carlton Mellick III** — Heaven is no longer a paradise. It was once a blissful utopia full of wonders far beyond human comprehension. But the afterlife is now in ruins. It has become an ugly, lonely wasteland populated by strange monstrous beasts, masturbating angels, and sad man-like beings wallowing in the remains of the once-great Kingdom of God. **106 pages $8**

BB-154 **"Space Walrus" Kevin L. Donihe** — Walter is supposed to go where no walrus has ever gone before, but all this astronaut walrus really wants is to take it easy on the intense training, escape the chimpanzee bullies, and win the love of his human trainer Dr. Stephanie. **160 pages $11**